Sing About It

Ursula Holden

Eyre Methuen

BY THE SAME AUTHOR

Endless Race
String Horses
Turnstiles
The Cloud Catchers
Penny Links

First published in Great Britain 1982 by
Eyre Methuen Ltd
11 New Fetter Lane, London EC4P 4EE
Copyright © 1982 Ursula Holden
Photoset and printed in Great Britain by
Redwood Burn Limited
Trowbridge, Wiltshire

British Library Cataloguing in Publication Data

Holden, Ursula
  Sing about it.
  I. Title
  823'.914[F]   PR6058.04/

ISBN 0–413–47730–4

❧ One

'Excuse me. Underwear?'

Sylvie had been buying presents in the high street for twenty years and seen changes. Large stores changed hands, the smaller ones merged or disappeared. The eastern world was merging with the west and life was uncertain. You saw uncertainty in everyone's eyes, you saw confusion. She noticed eyes. At Christmas eyes had less love, more suspicion, like puppets' eyes. The spirit of Christmas had weakened. Sylvie felt old, fat, out of it. The season had no joy any more. She'd buy something for herself first, before she bought for Tim. She had already overspent. Christmas carols were piped from the toy department, sounding about the store. The lights, the decorations, the noise wearied her. She was glad she wasn't a child today. She was glad that she had no child. Where were the home-made presents of childhood, the home-cooked food, the innocence? Her present to herself would be underwear.

'How much are those black lace pants?'

Loose-legged, diaphanous, in fashion again this year.

'Eight pounds, Madam.'

'Madam' was on the wane. 'Love' was more usual, spoken with insincerity.

'I'll try them please.' If they fitted she'd leave the old ones behind in the fitting-room.

She undressed. She heaved. They fitted. The elastic cut

her waist. Her figure saddened her now.

She pushed pound notes into the sales woman's hand. Her knickers would pass inspection. She walked through the toy department, disregarding toys, dolls, seasonal reminders. A human Santa leered from a tinfoil cave, a leer that turned to a grin when a mother paid the pound that opened his magic sack. Young and old enjoyed a spectacle. Toddlers were lifted to his knee to push hands in. Without a child she needn't join the sham. A shawled baby might be sweet though, or a young teenager. Too late for birth now. Sometimes she pretended Cap was her daughter. Buying alone was lonely. 'Oh little town of Bethlehem, How still we see thee lie, Above thy deep and dreamless sleep The silent stars go by.' Ignore toys and carols, head past the chemist counter out to the street. Something smells lovely, a cloying, sickly smell.

'What is that perfume please?'

'Our Christmas promotion. "Heart of a Rose." This, Madam, is the range.' Talcum powder, soaps, oils, all smelling beautiful. A rose was an emblem of love, though it meant 'horse' in Old High German. She'd buy some of the soap. A piece for Cap who lived where Sylvie worked, a piece for Tim. He would of course prefer to be given paints or brushes. Tim lived in a state of delusion about his talent, ignoring criticism as he hurled his paints about. If she complained he sulked, scowling his heavy brows. In his view early success bred early obscurity, though he was forty-six. She had admired him once. At their first meeting twenty-five years ago he had told her that he was Irish and that he painted. She had believed in him then. Her belief might have continued had she not won the football pools. He'd left his job then, shutting himself into the front room of their rented house to fling and daub full time. When the price of living increased she took the job to help boredom as well as finances. She'd ceased years ago to tell him lies about his talent, but nothing would stop him painting. The job

4

increased their comforts but not their happiness. She'd buy 'Heart of a Rose' soap to sweeten the lie of marriage. They didn't share a bed, had not seen each other naked for years. She felt more closeness with the residents of the Community where she worked, who owned nothing, who slept on mattresses on bare boards, than she felt with Tim. The residents liked and needed her for herself and not for the lies she told. 'Be good, be loving, you will find love in marriage,' was not for her. Too late to mourn the Christmases of childhood, the home-made cards, the candles, carols, gifts were gone. Her early dream of motherhood was just a dream. Now she was fat, spotty, disenchanted. She'd made her bed. Rose-smelling soaps, lace knickers were decades too late. She was still a good listener. 'I can talk to you. You understand. Look, Sylvie, I'm Irish and I paint,' he'd said on that first meeting. His voice had pleased her, his thrusting chin and dark brows pleased her. She'd stared, she had pretended, determining to become his wife. Now she was secondary to secondary work. He lacked any technique as he endlessly painted dogs. Too late now to change anything. The woman's movement had arrived too late for her. This Christmas she would concentrate on the residents. She'd already bought them a tree, crackers, little gifts. Her knickers cut her waist.

Outside the store she saw the man in the sandwich boards, walking a pace or two, stopping, head lowered like a mule. Each year he paced, advertising an umbrella sale. He paused by a window display of fur slippers. 'Walk warmly this Yuletide, be cosy on the day,' the golden placard read. The slippers mocked the man's own cracked shoes with scraps of sock showing. Sylvie felt something cold slithering along her thigh.

'Excuse me, you dropped something,' he whispered, his old face close to hers. Unable to stand upright he pointed to the ground where her new knickers lay in a black pool around her shoes. The waist elastic had snapped, leaving her bare and cold.

'My . . . hanky. Thank you.' She pushed them into her holdall, hoping he might think she was mourning a lost love, a black staunch for her tears.

'Take a good heart to life.'

'I will. I've seen you here before.'

'I have perambulated this stretch for thirty years. Or more probably.'

'Oh. Here is my bus. Goodbye.' She hoped he hadn't laughed. Unfashionable in her tight clothing she was as much a failure as her husband. She was a fraud too, pretending to be a community social worker, but she only had typing skills. She hoped that he would forget her, that they wouldn't meet again. The bus was full. Children clutched at parcels bought in Santa's cave. A toddler waved a glove puppet. A dog in a basket barked. She wished she had bought warm slippers for Cap. None of the residents of the Community of St Harmony owned proper footwear. She thought of the tree she had bought, hidden in the shed at home, its dark spikes smelling of ginger. The Community lacked essentials, they lacked curtains, carpets, heat. They'd have a pretty tree. She would call into St Harmony before she went back to Tim. St Harmony appreciated her.

'Cap. Cap, it's me, Sylvie. Open the door.'

'What you doing? I thought you was off duty.'

'I am. I've been shopping in the high street. I've bought something for you, something extra.'

'You buy something for the others too?'

'No. Just you.'

Sylvie had made biscuits and sweets for the residents, who had sweet tooths. These titbits were with the tree in the shed, to be brought over in the morning.

'What you want to go buying for me for? You ought to be back at your home.'

'I'm on my way there. My pants fell down in the street.'

'Stone the crows. I'll lend you something. I got something might fit you.'

'It's all right thank you. I'll wait till I get home. Open this.'

Cap turned the parcel over. She smelled the pink paper. 'Heart of a Rose,' she read slowly. She wasn't offended that Sylvie had refused her offer of clothes. Cap foraged in rubbish tips, in bins or on old building sites. Sometimes she bought clothing at jumble sales. Nothing was too dilapidated or dirty for her junk collection. What other people had least use for Cap collected. Her mattress was the worst in the Community. She kept an old car tyre in the middle of her room in which she stored her treasures. Her room was piled with rags, old shoes, boxes.

'Open the soap, Cap. It's pink.'

They sat on the tyre, squashing it with their weight. It made a sighing noise. Bottles, cracked plates and paper bags were round their feet. Cap grinned.

'Soap won't change me, Sylvie, I'll never change. I like old things, rags. You don't earn much, Warden don't pay a lot. Why waste your money on me?'

'I don't want you to change. I like giving you things. You don't have to use it.'

'You'll be moving in here next, getting so fond of the place. You ought to be at home.'

'If I wasn't married I might. I'm coming tomorrow. Warden is taking Christmas Day off.'

'Dirty old sod. He's looney, you know that?'

'He's good, but he's old. He can't help being old. What's in that red bag over there?'

'Just bits of make-up. I found them on a tip. Here, take it it's nail polish and stuff.'

Cap looked knowing. She knew Sylvie felt outcast, inexperienced in spite of her home and husband. She knew more about life at twenty, than Sylvie did at forty-four.

'I've never used make-up. I've always been so spotty.'

'We'll do our nails. Come on, a bit of paint works

wonders.'

Cap showed her. Three sweeps of the brush down each nail, wiping the tip clear. You had to blow to dry them, waving your fingers about. The acid pear-drop smell stung their eyes. Cap said there was eye make-up in the red bag too, they'd do their eyes next.

'I've never used mascara before. Cap, what's that noise? Who's that outside?'

'Most probably Mac. He's on the beer again I expect. Ignore him, it's Christmas.'

Someone was beating Cap's door. They heard Mac shouting then.

'Cap. Cap, I gorra have ashprin. Let me in, Cap. Ashprin.'

'You know I got nothink. Warden don't allow no pills, you know that, Mac.'

Drugs and alcohol were taboo at St Harmony, it was one of Warden Hemm's strictest rules. His residents were often weak-willed, with emotional troubles. Drugs of any kind were dangerous, could lead to trouble. He gave them shelter, he wouldn't allow gambling. He liked his residents to keep active, to avoid emotional entanglements. In return for board and lodging he expected their co-operation. Sylvie supported his rules. She was afraid of drunks, of anything abnormal. She didn't want to let Mac in. Cap could deal best with him. The two were friends. She waved her painted nails, knowing Cap knew of her fear.

'Keep quiet. Ignore him. You ain't supposed to be here anyway, it's your day off. He wants aspirin 'cos he's pissed. He wants some kind of pill. Hold still, Sylvie, while I paint your eyes.'

Cap twirled the brush round the inside of the bottle. Sylvie was silly, buying presents she couldn't afford, silly being afraid of Mac. That's what a sheltered background did to you. She'd improve Sylvie's face for her at any rate.

'Cap don't poke my eye out. Don't. My god, Cap, what

8

are you doing? What have you done? Cap, what have you done to my eye?'

Her right eye stung, a sting increasing to pain. She saw red shapes. She screamed. Cap had blinded her right eye.

'I made a mistake, Sylvie. I got mixed up. Look, Sylv, red everywhere. I got the bottles mixed. Gawd, you're all red.'

Nail varnish dripped over Cap's tennis shoes, ran down the cracks in the tyre. Sylvie rubbed her eye, her hand came away red. She'd be blinded, her sight would go, she'd never see properly again. She felt for her holdall, her shoes slipped in the red. She must leave before anything worse happened, she must get away. Leave the Community to their rag-picking, their drinking and failed fates. She pushed past Mac in the hall, she felt him clutching her, she pushed him back. Leave him, bang the door. She might never see properly again. From somewhere in the community a small voice sang. 'Oh little town of Bethlehem.' Leave them, get away.

'Sylvie, you're late. The shops have closed hours ago. What's wrong with your eye? That's not blood is it? Dear *me*.'

'An accident at St Harmony. Some nail varnish got spilled.'

'But why were you there? This is your day off. You spend too much time there. That place is no good for you.'

'But Tim, they need me.'

'It's Christmas Eve. *I* need you. I need you to clean my brushes for me. My palette knife is lost. Since you've worked at that place you've lost any sense of responsibility.'

'But they need me. I am committed.'

'And me? I need my tea. You should feel committed to me. The light is gone, I can't paint any more. You waste too much time. Do wash your face, your eye looks quite un-pleasant.'

She went up to the bathroom to run cold water over her face. She made his tea then.

❧ Two

Her head ached in the morning because she hadn't slept. Tim had slept soundly. She covered her right eye, then her left, looking towards the window. She could see from both eyes but her right vision was blurred, things looked distorted. Last night she'd made Tim worry, he'd come upstairs after her, had stood outside the bathroom ill at ease while she ran cold water. His worry hadn't lasted. Now it was Christmas morning. She lay still.

'There now, you can see can't you? No harm done. I wondered last night if you should see a doctor. I can get him if you wish.'

'Not on Christmas Day. I'll bathe them again, and Warden has some eye ointment. I'll get some when I go over later.'

Any concern he might feel was lost in another fit of annoyance.

'You're surely not going back. Not today, I won't have it, Sylvie.'

'I must. I told you, Warden has gone away. He's gone to the West Country, somebody must be in charge.'

'Why you? He should be there, not you. He works you too hard, Sylvie.'

'You know we take turns at holiday times. I like working.'

He'd not bothered to wish her a happy Christmas. She

didn't expect a present.

'You're not fit to work, I think you ought to rest. I wish you had taken more care. Look . . . shall I make some tea?'

She watched him, one hand over her eye as he bumped the tray awkwardly. He'd combed curls of fading dark hair over his balding patch. He'd shaved carelessly, wisps of cotton wool stuck to his jutting chin. He bought in two cards from the letterbox.

'One is from Warden, the other one from Cap.' She wished he'd asked her about her shopping trip. She would have liked to have told him about her adventures in the high street. She knew he wanted to return to the dead dog he was painting as soon as possible. She thought again of childhood, of hearing carols, of holding toys and smelling spicy foods.

'Happy Christmas, Tim. I bought something for you.'

'Thanks very much, Sylvie. Sorry I bought you nothing, we don't usually bother with gifts. I've been too busy.'

'It's only something small.'

'What's this? Soap? Look, would you like me to cook lunch?'

He sniffed the soap, uncomfortable, wanting to make amends.

She said he could if he wished, there were tins in the cupboard, they could have a snack early, before she left for work. He looked relieved that the meal would be simple. He was trying to placate her, normally he liked his food. He'd said nothing more about her leaving him in favour of that place. He avoided using the name 'St Harmony', preferring to say 'that place'. There was no saint by that name. The name was fake, the place was fake, owned by a fake character who worked his wife too hard. Because of 'that place' he'd have to cook his own dinner, forego a proper meal. He'd take a bet that she'd laid in proper food for *them*, while he had to make do with soup.

She lay listening to him moving about below. He clattered tin openers, dropped a plate, cursing. The smell was like burning cabbage. She'd loved cooking for him once, a long time ago. The boredom she now felt in her kitchen matched the boredom of marriage. Sleeping accommodation had been no problem since their honeymoon. She'd longed then for her single bed, had longed to get back to it. She'd felt dry, nervous, stiff. She'd never had an orgasm. It had been single beds ever since. They'd not kissed since the honeymoon. She admired Cap who had no fear, much experience. Cap did as she pleased with everyone and led a hedonist life. When she felt like fun she went with Mac to the West End of London. She picked up men while Mac drank, the two returning refreshed. They never asked Sylvie to go with them, nor did they speak of these trips. Mac collected knives. At night he could be heard throwing them in his room. He hadn't been long at the Community, had arrived drunk, his only possession a pocket knife.

Something smells lovely,' she called, falsely.

'I found a tinned pudding in the cupboard.'

'You could pour brandy over it, to celebrate.'

Neither drank alcohol. Brandy was kept in the bathroom for emergencies. Bored with each other, without children to liven the home, their day would be marked by brandy poured over a tin of pudding. The soup he brought her tasted of dog food. He'd made slices of blackened toast. She quite liked the pudding, though he refused any. He'd indulged her whim for brandy over treacle sponge, he wanted to paint now.

'Let's have a drink in bed.' She didn't know why she said it, she didn't want him near her, didn't want him touching. She wished they didn't even share a room. Tim used the smaller bedroom to store work in, his work of twenty odd years. Various shaped dogs in various sizes were stacked there from floor to ceiling. He wouldn't part with one. Since the honeymoon their beds had been separated by a night table. It would take more than brandy to unite them, nor did she wish such a unity. They were embarrassed. He frowned, not answering. They were relieved when the doorbell rang and he could leave the room. She heard him speak to the caller, his brogue more pronounced because of his embarrassment.

'We come to see Sylvie. She all right?' She was expected round at Harm's.'

'Cap. Come upstairs. I'm here.'

Sylvie smelled Cap and Mac before they got into the room, a thick sad smell of old clothes. Their knees bumped the bed. Mac hunched his broad shoulders uneasily, not used to seeing Sylvie away from the Community.

'Tim wanted me to stay in bed. I'm coming to work later. Is everything all right?'

'I've looked after them, don't you worry. Has Tim been looking after you?' Cap didn't trust Tim. She knew what he thought of St Harmony, knew that he didn't make Sylvie happy. She thought his paintings abominable. If he had to paint dogs, why not living ones?

'I'm doing all that is necessary, thank you very much.' Tim straightened her eiderdown, then fussed with the curtains. The couple from that place were all that was needed to ruin his day.

'She needs visitors. She got a rotten fright. What did you give her for dinner?'

'Soup. Tim gave me soup. And brandy on the pudding. Thank you for your card, Cap.' They'd cared enough to visit her. Her spirits rose. Mac was quite sober, his eyes gentle and caring.

'Come home with us now,' he said.

'I will. I'm coming later. I'm bringing a surprise.'

'What surprise might that be, Sylvie?' Tim saw now why they'd eaten such a poor lunch. She'd overspent the housekeeping, buying surprises for that lot. She was besotted enough about them to subsidise their lack of funds. Slum lot. He took a poor view of dropouts dropping into his home, breaking the seasonal peace. That lad couldn't be much over twenty and he reeked of liquor. The girl was no better than a gypsy. Sylvie oughtn't to go with them, she ought to stay with him. She was becoming an unwise secretive spender. He left them to go downstairs to the front room and his dog canvas. They heard him put it on the floor. He did that sometimes in order to aim paint more accurately.

The visitors looked meaningfully at Sylvie. 'Come home,' Mac said again.

'You better get there soon, Sylvie. We got a new resident. He come last night after Warden left.' Cap picked up Tim's untasted pudding, she handed it to Mac who spooned the sponge into his mouth. Cap gathered the plates up. She knew when a home had happiness. She blamed Sylvie for much of the trouble. You had to be tough with men, husbands especially, you had to demand your rights. A married woman should insist on comfort. Things like wrought-iron touches, a bit of green in front, porch lanterns mattered. Sylvie hadn't learned the rules, though she had a lot to put up with. She'd seen the latest dog canvas on her way up the stairs. She'd not rescue it from a dump. Tim was a man with problems. He never laughed either.

'I'll follow on. You go back now, Cap. Somebody should be there with them, especially today. Thank you both for coming to see me.'

Despite bitten nails, tennis shoes and dirt, Cap had enchantment, moving with sluttish grace. Her mouth was pinched, covering uneven teeth, her eyes were rather bulbous but she had confidence. She believed she was always right, she believed she was glamorous.

Sylvie went to the shed, pulling her parcels out. She unwrapped the tree from its newspaper. She asked Tim for some of the gold paint she'd got for him. He was fond of painting with gold, highlighting his dogs' eyes and whiskers as well as gold for the frames.

14

'What for? Gold is expensive.'

'I need it to paint this tree. I bought the paint, I earned the money. I want to paint this tree.'

She took one of his brushes, she painted the tree rapidly. Gold dripped from the boughs, dripping across her shoes. Tim watched her from the doorway, his eyes angry, hard. While the paint dried she packed her gifts into the holdall. She must get there quickly, Cap ought not to be left alone, she was only a resident like the others, in need of care like the others.

'I won't be late home. See you tonight, Tim.'

'Tonight? It's Christmas Day, Sylvie. Have I no rights, no importance for you? That lot don't want you. I do, what about my tea?' Anger roughened his voice. She was without a conscience, the creature. Parvenue. How did she dare?

'It's my work, I keep telling you. They're my job. A new intake is waiting. Cap shouldn't be left alone.'

'Her? That one? She should be left alone entirely. Are you angry because I bought you nothing? Getting your own back at me?'

'I didn't expect anything. My job is my life.'

'*My* job is my life, my painting. Those dropouts don't know one day from another. They don't want or need you.'

'You're wrong. They need friendship.'

'What use are they? They contribute nothing. Drain fodder, puppet figures. You go showering them with gold trees, liberality. Why bother?'

'They're worth bothering with. I need them. It's not as if we had children, or any proper friends. They are my friends.'

'Children? That's right drag that in. Is that my fault, am I to blame? You ... you ...'

'We're married Tim, but not in a real sense. I don't think we ever were. We're just a habit for each other. When did you do more than touch my eiderdown? When did you care what I thought? You give me orders, when did you give *me* thought?'

She remembered his disgust, her shame and shyness when she had a period on their honeymoon. He'd started his dead animal paintings from that time. A life of bolted bathroom doors, silences, never touching bodily wasn't as bad as never touching mentally.

She went out into the bitter cold. Her true Christmas was starting now, with a long parcel under her arm and gifts in her holdall. Tim wouldn't spoil her day. Mac who liked whisky and knives and Cap in her room full of rags were waiting.

※ Three

The porch roof of St Harmony sagged. A plank hung loose giving the house a ruffian look. The windows looked like opened eyes, the doorway a waiting muzzle. Sylvie ran up the steps.

Warden Hemm tried to be strict about rules. The residents knocked for admittance, demanding bed and board. He asked for co-operation, rarely getting it. The residents broke locks and windows for no reason. The telephone suffered the most. Breakages were worst when Warden wasn't there. Inside the hall was colder than it was outside, a silent, waiting cold. The doors leading from the hall were closed, except for the office where Warden's telephone was ripped from the wall again. Only Warden slept on an official bed in his bedroom leading from the office. His door-handle was smashed. Sylvie wasn't surprised at the breakages. She rapped at Cap's door again.

'I'm here again, Cap. I've brought the surprise.'

Someone had left a sandwich on the floor by the staircase, a small triangular bite from it showing an edging of cheese. She heard Cap's tennis shoes scuffing again. When she opened the door the room looked even worse than yesterday. She stared at Sylvie as if she didn't recognize her. Her bulging eyes under her unparted hair were blank. Her hair stuck out from a central point like a twig broom. She never used her comb. The residents had short memories, spells of

17

amnesia were common, an effect, Sylvie supposed, of the life they'd had previously. She had got used to blank looks and forgetfulness

'I told you I'd come. I'm here. My present is this tree.'

'We don't need no tree here.'

'Look at it, Cap. I painted it myself. Isn't it beautiful.'

'You got gold over your shoes. It's snowing in the west, where Warden went.'

'His telephone is slashed through again, someone has hacked the flex. Who did it, do you know?'

A broken transistor radio lay on its side in the middle of Cap's tyre. Cap stared past Sylvie at the tree standing on the tennis table in the hall. She smiled then, not caring about the telephone. She stretched her hand out.

'A tree ain't no use without decorations.'

'I've brought decorations. In the holdall.'

'Bells. Stars. All them tinsels. Stone the crows, Sylvie, you spent a lot.'

'I wanted it to be perfect. Is Mac in?'

'He's in his room. He's practising with his knives. Listen.'

They heard small thudding sounds hitting against Mac's door, and then voices.

'Who is he with?'

'Don't bother about Mac. Let's look at the decorations.'

Cap picked the gold baubles from the holdall, the birds, stars, flowers and musical instruments, turning them in her hands, marvelling.

Mac came out then, a calculating look in his eye. He looked pleased to see Sylvie.

'You came then, Sylvie. That tree is nice. Did you bring it?'

He touched the decorations. He said the birds were lyre birds, he'd read about them.

The residents were poor scholars. The local libary had barred them from membership because they abused the

18

service, spoiling books, failing to return them. Cap collected newspapers and old comics which they looked at. You could scribble and tear them with a free hand.

'Look. Fairies,' Mac said.

'Them is angels, Mac, not fairies. Look, here is more.'

'About this new resident, Cap. Who is he? We're full already, you know that.'

St Harmony had four bedrooms leading off the hall. The floor above was too derelict to use. No one used the stairs if they could avoid them, they stuck to the kitchen and hall. The hall was bare except for the tennis table. There was no floor covering.

'He's old. I couldn't say no.'

'How old? Warden isn't keen on having geriatrics. They get ill.'

'Suit yourself then. It ain't my job to pry, I never asked his age. Is your eye better?'

'Things look a bit shadowy. It keeps watering. It's nothing serious.'

'You wearing them pants I gave you? I bet you threw them away didn't you? I bet Tim didn't buy you nothing either.'

'We don't give presents, we don't bother. Thank you for your card. I'll leave the tree on the table here where people can see it coming in. What is the newcomer's name?'

'I took him in. It ain't my job to fill in files, that's Warden's job. You know how he is about the files.'

'Which room is he in? Did he go upstairs?'

'It isn't safe, you know that. Mr Silk let him have his room. Mr Silk moved in with Mac. Mac offered, didn't you, Mac? Mac's sharing with Mr Silk.'

'That's nice of you, Mac. Especially at Christmas. I thought I heard voices.'

'He needed a room. No bother.'

'What's Christmas got to do with it? We don't need Christmas here, we don't care, not here.'

No one liked giving up space or privacy. Sharing was not encouraged by Warden Hemm. Sharing aggravated quarrelling. His residents needed solitude and quiet for their troubled minds. Each was responsible for his own room. Warden didn't visit the bedrooms unless invited. In his view too much interaction was worse than too little. He kept notes in their files, charting behaviour and progress. Once a file was opened only Warden touched it. Top secret, they were for his eyes only. One of Sylvie's jobs was to make out a file when somebody new arrived. No use scolding Cap, she'd done as she thought best. Mr Silk and Mac were an ill-assorted pair. Mac with his love of knives and whisky was unpredictable. Mr Silk was something of a mystic. Mac put down the lyre birds, going back to his room. The heard the quiet thud of his knives.

'Cap, I wish I were as thin as you. I wish I were young again.'

'You ain't old, you just feel it. Do you still get monthlies?'

'Not for a while. I never notice dates.'

'Take care not to get pregnant. Now don't go all bashful, Sylv. Anyone would think you was a virgin.'

'I'm not bashful.'

'Tim is a funny bloke. You two don't laugh much do you? Your house is miserable.'

Sylvie looked at her fingers. She spoke quietly. Tim hated touching her, she thought he hated her. With nothing in common their life together was farcical. He only cared about paint. What could she do?

'Try making him jealous. Those single beds don't help either. You want him don't you?'

'I don't know.'

'You're a bit old to start again now. You ought to laugh. People don't laugh enough.'

Cap told her that men needed to feel important, wanted. You had to study them if you fancied keeping them. The poor sods were made like that, wanting their own way. Most people were selfish. Cap favoured the single life herself, didn't fancy getting wed. Sylvie should cheer herself up. Fatness and old age happened to everyone. Fun mattered, a bit of life, some laughs.

Sylvie longed to be like Cap who only owned rubbish and enjoyed herself. She would go now to welcome the newcomer who was probably feeling strange.

Mr Silk had the largest room. His window let in the sun. He'd painted a dragon on the centre panel of his door. She didn't expect an answer to her knock. Residents tended to withdraw when they arrived. She turned the handle. The room inside was changed, no trace of Mr Silk left. It was empty except for a tall figure in the window. He turned. It was the man with the sandwich boards that she'd seen yesterday standing outside the store. He stared unrecognizingly, his pupils barely showing beneath slack upper lids. His eyeballs were veined with red. His boards were propped against the windowsill, the gold lettering catching the light. 'Umbrellas old, umbrellas new, hand over cash, keep dry in lieu.' Mr Silk's nice utensils, his wall-hangings from eastern parts and his carved figurine were gone. No sandalwood scented the air. The bent old man didn't move. A household cat slipped in behind Sylvie to rub up against the boards.

'Hello. We already met. We met yesterday didn't we? This is a nice surprise.'

'I . . .'

'I'm Sylvie. I'm the social worker here.'

'I beg your pardon?'

'I said I'm Sylvie. I've come to welcome you. How did you hear about St Harmony?'

'I received information from . . . Where is this?'

'The Community of St Harmony owned and run by Warden Hemm. I work here for Warden. I've come for your particulars. Each resident has a file which Warden

21

keeps. A private record of achievement and progress. Now, your name, and where did you live previously?'

Warden liked as much information as possible. Jobs previously held and former addresses were sometimes hard to obtain. She was used to newcomers arriving confused, unsure of anything. A name, a date of birth slipped the memory when you needed a room desperately, some peace and quiet. She felt hard-hearted but she needed to know. The newcomer gave a worried look at the cat sniffing his sandwich boards.

'Life is a lottery. Is this a place of worship?'

'This is St Harmony. I saw you yesterday, remember? I saw you in the street. What is your name?' She didn't want him to remember her black knickers that she'd pretended were a hanky. His mind seemed far away. He spoke with a precise accent.

'I'm . . . I am Every.'

'Welcome to St Harmony, Every. You will be happy here when you get used to it. This room did belong to Mr Silk, the sunniest room in the house. He came from the east. He's moved in to share with Mac. We'll find a mattress for you. It's a bit rough and ready but all right. Have you any clothes? Any luggage anywhere?'

'I beg your pardon?'

'Possessions. Don't worry. It doesn't matter.'

He looked more solitary standing in Mr Silk's room than he had in the bitter street. His arms stuck stiffly, his coat was too big. His mauve mouth had no teeth. It was impossible to imagine him as a young man, virile, breaking hearts. It was possible that he was shamming amnesia or deafness to avoid being questioned. Then he spoke hurriedly.

'How old would you say I was?'

'Fifty-eight? Early sixties?' He looked older. The residents liked flattery, she'd soon found that out.

'Wrong. Forty-eight. I'm fitter than I seem. Fresh air, that is my secret. I work in the open air.' He grinned quickly, a gnome sharing a secret.

'You look well. A bit tired perhaps. Are you keeping your job on?'

'It is my intention.'

She explained that those who didn't work at jobs outside were expected to help in the house. St Harmony functioned on democratic lines. Warden tried to create a family atmosphere. She tried to make her voice enthusiastic. Few residents ever pulled their weight. Left to herself Cap could be helpful; by nature she was lazy, indifferent, putting pleasure first. Nobody attended the house meetings that Warden held every week. Nobody mended broken things round the house. Warden had an uphill task. Only Mac admitted to loving St Harmony.

'I never missed a day's employment in forty years. I take a good heart. Is this residence quiet? I'm not a lover of cats you understand?'

'On the whole it is. Sometimes they quarrel. We always need help in the kitchen.'

'I'm not a lover of kitchen work. They quarrel did you say?'

As if in answer a crash came from the hall making them jump. Thumping, shouting, smashing of glass, the sound of a body crashing. Sylvie hated fights. She was in charge and Warden was far away. The residents were harder to control when he wasn't there; they were in awe of him, though they mocked and ignored his rules. Every trembled.

'I'd better go to them. I'm in charge. They'll hurt each other, let go of me.'

'Don't leave me. Don't.'

'I must. I told you, Warden isn't here.'

'This is a house of madness.' He spoke flatly, resigned. There was another thud, more shouting.

'They sometimes fight. It's Christmas day you see. Let go of me please, Every.'

His fingers round her elbow felt like bones. She heard

Cap then, blessed Cap who wasn't afraid of fights. Cap could hit, shout, kick anyone into behaving better. They heard her shouting at Mac to stop it. To put away his knife, leave Mr Silk alone.

'Knives? They are mad here,' Every said.

'No, just arguing, a friendly fight I expect.'

They listened again. Home-loving Mac and Mr Silk were fighting about sharing. Mr Silk objected to Mac's knives.

'I am a man of peace. No weapons in room of meditation.'

'But you didn't have to put a cat on my mattress. Dirty animal,' Mac growled.

'Animal not dirtee. I show respect to beast. No violence.'

'It messed my mattress. I'll slit its throat if you let it in again.'

Every seemed to shrink inside his coat. The cost of admission was high. Cats, fighting, knives and madness.

Sylvie opened his door. Cap stood in the hall by the golden tree on the tennis table. Her bulging eyes were angry. The two men were fussing over nothing. There was nothing wrong with a cat. Mac's knife collection was harmless, nothing wrong with a hobby. She held Mr Silk by his cotton sleeve. Mac waved his knife, the nostrils of his broad nose widening with upset. There was the noise of cats.

'Oh do stop everyone. It's Christmas, you shouldn't fight.'

Cap explained loudly that Mr Silk started the argument. He'd put a cat on the bed on purpose to torment Mac.

'Did you, Mr Silk?'

No one at St Harmony had seen him upset before. His hands, usually clasped in peace over his stomach, were tense, his mouth was straight above his gold-filled teeth, his unusually blue eyes were slitted deep into his head.

'I will not sleep with barbarian. Mac dangerous fellow.'

'Then why did you give up your room? You must have known he had knives, that he likes throwing them.'

Mr Silk shook his head miserably. He hadn't known, he was used to staying apart, meditating in his sunny room.

'He put that cat in purposely. I won't have it on my bed, flea-bitten thing,' Mac snarled.

'Not dirtee. Noble beast.'

'I wish I hadn't said I'd share. I'll slit it from north to south. I'll make you pay and all. Bloody oriental.'

'I eat. I pray. I give up room. End of subject.'

Tears fell over his cotton coat. They were against him, they were racially prejudiced. When they insulted him they insulted his nice utensils, his mat, his wall-hangings and figurine. He'd been called names in front of a stranger, he'd been made to lose face. His good act wasn't appreciated. He wanted his old room back, the sunny one.

'You shouldn't have been put together. There are more rooms upstairs.' Sylvie spoke doubtfully. The rooms were damp, with guttering outside that leaked. The stairs leading to them were weak in places. The downstairs rooms, though cold, were weatherproof. Not even Ruffler the Australian, who was a short-stay visitor, used any rooms upstairs. He preferred rolling his swag out under the tennis table. Sole, who only came to stay in winter, had no bedroom either, but put his mattress anywhere in any odd corner.

'How many reside here?' Every's mouth dropped with dismay, his bare gums showed.

'The permanents are me, Mac, Mr Silk. Sole comes and goes in summer. Sylvie works here, she doesn't stop, she has a husband at home. Ruffler is only stopping for the night. We can't use upstairs, Sylvie, it's rotten, it ain't safe, Sylvie.'

'What will become of me? I show respect to peoples. Must I share with barbarian?'

'Watch out who you're calling names,' Mac snarled. His face looked suddenly drunk again. Like all of them his moods changed quickly. Grievances and joys didn't last

25

long, though Mr Silk was known for serenity. Some thought he had a wife in Hyderabad or some mysterious eastern part. He'd once whispered to Sylvie that he'd lost loved ones in war, was giving his life to peace. He abstained from meat as well as eschewing violence. He had grounds for objecting to knives.

'Listen, it's Christmas, you haven't noticed the tree. We'll decorate it. I bought things with me. Things to eat, and lights.'

'I've seen the ornaments. Fairies, I mean angels, and birds. Lyre birds they are.' Mac made a pass with his knife over the top of the tree.

'Careful, Mac, don't knock it.'

'Ring for the police,' moaned Mr Silk wringing his lemon-toned hands.

'You can't. The phone is broke.'

Cap picked up a golden angel. Two bells and a bird had fallen to the floor. Sylvie opened the sweets. Sweet things would soothe their mood, sweet things would make them smile. Mac put his knife down. The cat with the stumpy tail paused, one paw raised while the sweet wrappings rustled. Cap reached for a liqueur chocolate wrapped in bottle-shaped foil. There was quiet, then a sound of sucks as they all sucked sweet drink out of chocolate bottles.

'This is no Christian establishment,' Every mumbled. But he liked chocolate as much as anyone.

'It is in principle. Warden's ideas are based on unselfishness. It is a charity.'

No one knew his exact denomination, nor did they care. They thought Warden rather a mug, working without thanks or reward.

'Where is the crib?'

'There isn't one. But Warden reads tracts every day. He's quite a Christ-like man.'

When Sylvie knew Warden was reading she tried to keep the residents away from the office. He shouldn't be disturbed. Cap afforded him the least respect, she gossiped about him, said he was a fraud or on the make. Now she picked over the chocolates, looking for a whisky one for Mac.

'We all need Warden. Without him you wouldn't have a roof. I wouldn't have a job without him.'

'We'd manage. There are other jobs.'

'I am a Buddhist,' said Mr Silk. He found the tree pleasing, all gold and harmonious. He wasn't one to harbour grudges, he'd think about those sharp knives later. He bent to stroke a cat.

'Who broke the phone I wonder. I've got a good idea. Come on out, Babe, come on, come to Cap.' Cap rapped the door under the stairs.

Every's mauve lips dropped again. This was the final straw. He could accept a bare broken house, fighting, cats messing, violence by knife. He should have been warned that a woman three and a half feet tall would walk out from under the stairs. She walked lurchingly, her twisty legs moving with difficulty. She wore gaiters to conceal her bowed calves that looked almost circular, and small galoshes on her feet. She stumbled into Cap's arms. He wondered if Cap had forgotten to mention this person or if she'd left her out in deference to her shyness.

'This is Loveliness,' Sylvie told him.

Loveliness didn't like noise. She didn't like being stared at. Stares made her nervous. She slept on a doll's bed under the stairs, spending a lot of time there. She usually ate alone. Warden had a soft spot for her. She was the darling of Cap but not well liked by Sylvie. She spent long hours under the stairs looking at her scrapbooks which recorded her years working in a circus. During the war when talent had been short Loveliness had been famous. Dressed in white swansdown she rode round the ring in a pumpkin coach drawn by a team of dogs. Or she had popped from an Easter egg wearing white bunnies' ears. She had even swung from a crescent moon in a costume that concealed her legs. Captions described her antics. 'Loveliness Marker goes to the ball.' 'Miss Marker visits rabbit land, love is born at Eastertide.' 'Sweet and Loveliness goes moon riding, flying to the man of her dreams.' After the war no one wanted her. There were those with more than an upper half to show, who could leap and tumble and reveal comic skills. Now she lived with her memories and pictures, smiling and looking at herself. She was spoiled by Cap and Warden, she had been there longer than the rest. She was a pensioner.

She twined her legs round Cap's waist. Every closed his mouth. He was used to the unexpected when he was walking the streets inside his sandwich boards, but those legs looping the rag-and-bone girl's waist weren't something seen every day. Her hair was arranged in a style of forty years ago. Pinkish-grey make-up clogged her wrinkles.

'What's happening? What's up? Manners please. Introductions.' Loveliness had a twittery voice.

'This is the newcomer, Babe, the one what come last night. We've been having a fight about rooms. You heard it didn't you? Hey mister, what's this your name is?'

'Every.' He tried to bow. His back hurt. He tried to look gentlemanly.

'I'm Loveliness Marker. Do you believe in womanly liberation?'

'I beg your parden?'

'Babe, he isn't interested in your politics. Every is a funny name for a person. Look Babe, what Sylvie bought.'

'I heard. I heard. Quite sweet I'm sure.'

'We're going to decorate. Now then, don't choke on that.'

Loveliness had grabbed the chocolates, was sucking a bottle loudly. Mr Silk chose a crème de menthe one. He smiled. The golden tree was a truce, festivity brought cordiality. The newcomer was a venerable man.

28

'Let's welcome Every officially. He only came last night.'

'Welcome Venerable to our bough of peace.'

'How do. I hope you don't mind knives.'

'Merry Christmas I'm sure. Do you fancy the circus?'

'Muck in at Harm's with us. You don't want to pay no mind to Mac and Mr Silk fighting.'

They were doing their best to be welcoming. Sylvie felt quite proud. Every pulling himself tall told them he used to carve wood. He might make a crib for the household, that's if they were Christian.

'We don't care one way or the other. Please yourself.'

Loveliness slid from Cap's arms to get beneath the lower branches of the tree. A gold angel touched her hair. The others looked at the decorations wonderingly, turning them in the light. When they had finished one box of sweets they started another. They liked them very much. Mr Silk went to Mac's bedroom to fetch some of his joss sticks. Smoke wound round their heads and got in their eyes, softening their lost expressions. Eyes showed when you had been unwanted, a look that lasted a long time. They kept dropping the decorations; it seemed silly to hang them on the tree, they looked pretty on the floor. Ruffler the Australian came in, followed by Sole who came and went in summer. The party was complete, except for Warden Hemm away in the West Country. Ruffler had a harmonica in his swag under the tennis table, Cap had some sparkler fireworks. There were just two left. She gave one to Loveliness, pet of the party, the other to Every, newcomer and old. He forgot to cover his gums, jabbing his sparkler to make sparks fly round their hair. Loveliness pretended to write her name, making an 'L' in the air while Ruffler blew a few notes. Harsh words were forgotten.

'What is your job, Every? You going out to work or stopping here at home?' Cap liked to be in the know. She was concerned for all the residents. She suspected that Every might be a bit loopy.

'It's all right, Cap. I've started making his file out, I'm taking his particulars.'

'I can ask, can't I? I let the bugger in.'

Ruffler blew loudly, a sustained note. Every glared at Cap.

'I . . . am . . . in . . . advertising.'

'Theatreland? The halls?' Loveliness blushed. She said she'd been in showbiz herself.

'Balls. He's never been in the halls. He ain't no actor, pull the other one.'

'That is enough, Miss,' Loveliness hissed. Every might be her ticket of intro, the means to her comeback. One telephone call could do it, change her life backwards. Cap shouldn't be rude. Cap was jealous, not wanting her to star again.

'Not the halls. Sandwich boards are my line, used rainwear my commodity. I work in the open air for an umbrella firm.'

'My my. Degrading. But are you a womanly libber?' Loveliness licked chocolate from a doll sized thumb.

'That's a tough job, Every,' Cap said with sympathy. No wonder the sod looked worn. She'd been quite right to take him in, old as he was.

'Western weather inclement,' Mr Silk murmured.

'It is my occupation. I'm a fit man.'

'This is your home now.' Mac aimed his knife at the stump-tailed cat to frighten it.

'May I enquire if this property is condemned?' Every couldn't stop looking at Loveliness. She was a small bad dream.

'It's Warden's property. He is a kindly man.' Sylvie wanted to reassure him.

'Not a squat?'

'Squat? You calling us squatters? Where have you been, with the meths men?'

'Mac is teasing, Every. Don't take him seriously.'

30

'I'm not teasing. The bugger smells. Why does he keep staring?'

'I'm not staying in these premises to be insulted. Allow the eastern gentleman to reoccupy his room. I will leave.'

'Please please don't take offence. We want you, Every,'

'Let Venerable Every stay. My room of peace is his. No problem. End of subject.'

'Stay, Every. Sorry I was rude. Show me your sandwich boards. I'll show you my knives.'

'Merry Christmas. Merry Christmas.' Loveliness liked a bit of argy-bargy, especially when she had sweets.

Ruffler rooted in his swag to find a pack of cards. They liked to play Happy Families, a simple childish game. The tree lights didn't work, they peered at their cards by the light of the sixty watt bulb, sitting on the floor among the fallen decorations.

'Show us your belly dance, Mr Silk,' Loveliness called boldly.

He looked pained. He was a modest man, not given to showing off. He stood. 'Good people. I show exercising.'

He lowered his head, having removed his shoes. He clasped his hands on the floor, his expression remaining sweet. He raised his heels over his shoulders. There was silence. His paunch hung down in line with his chest and chin. No one had seen this before, he was meditating publicly. They closed in. He flashed his gold-capped teeth at them, squinting his very blue eyes. He crossed his stockinged feet, pushing his elbows to raise his head from the floor. They begged him to show them more.

'I teach truth. Breathe. Conquer self.'

'Why? What is so good about breathing? We're breathing all the time. I like myself. I don't want to conquer it.' Cap argued, not agreeing at all. She tried to copy him, falling, showing her grubby underclothes. Ruffler blew his harmonica again. Mac waved his knife. Sole sat cracking his knuckles. Sylvie gathered up the playing cards. They'd

31

nearly finished the liqueur sweets.

Every felt confident, he spoke in an important tone. 'As I was saying I am a lover of wood. It has to be good wood, that's if you want a crib. There again I could carve a crucifix.'

They were all too engrossed to notice Warden's brown and white beard at the doorway. Loveliness still sat under the tree. 'Oh little town of Bethlehem, How still we see thee lie, Above thy deep and dreamless sleep The silent stars go by.'

❧ Four

Nothing was said until the next day. On Boxing Day morning Warden asked Sylvie into his office. He sat at his trestle table staring at his broken telephone, his silver-topped cane by his side. He wore his military coat; his eye sockets were withered with cold. His hair was an unreal nut-coloured brown; he'd forgotten to touch up his beard. With an angry look he squared his shoulders, waiting for Sylvie to speak.

'You surprised us yesterday, Warden, we weren't expecting you. Did you enjoy the West Country?'

He spoke in a tight voice about dedication to duty, of standards in etiquette. He'd worried about the Community, he'd cut his holiday short because they were on his mind. The drive back had been tiresome. He spoke of road blocks, of the death of animals, of cars abandoned in snow drifts. He'd been inconvenienced, endured discomfort, had had no holiday rest. What he had seen on his arrival was worst than anything he'd endured while away. Cards. Alcohol, dissipation, the flouting of everything that St Harmony stood for. He'd opened his door and seen. His rules, they had broken his rules.

'Only a bit of fun, Warden, we weren't doing anything wrong. The residents were enjoying themselves in quite a harmless way. They enjoy a bit of life.'

The skin over his cheekbones coloured. He was a frail

man with a limp. His brown tweed suit, his brogues with fringed tongues over knitted socks clothed rather ageing bones. Near his cane was his briefcase containing the residents' files that he kept with him always. Every closed dossier was in front of him. His tracts were in the briefcase too, his tracts that refreshed and encouraged him. He loved high-minded precepts, documentation, rules. The residents needed rules, a disciplined routine.

'But I saw, Sylvie. I saw smoke, alcohol, gambling, saw with my own eyes.'

'The smoke was from joss sticks or fireworks. They had sweets not alcohol, sweets shaped like bottles. We weren't gambling, we had Happy Families, a game that Ruffler has. I do uphold your rules.'

'Sylvie. Sylvie.' Warden felt confused. It troubled him that he'd not been so alert recently. He tired quickly, could he be losing his grip? He'd started the community with the highest hopes. Regimentation was the stuff of life though so far his hopes of introducing squad drilling and fatigue parties hadn't been realized. He blamed Sylvie for much of his failure. Sometimes he felt she was scarcely better than the ones she'd been hired to help. He'd advertised the post three years ago. 'Capable woman required for a Community of destitute and troubled souls. Qualifications less important than heart.' She'd been the only applicant. She had appeared suitable, he liked her homeliness and the fact that she lived near by. But she'd let him down often, she was too soft and weak. His west country trips were his tonic. His tracts, *Striving To Grow, In Search of Unity* and *Flog and Slog* helped him too.

'I'm sorry, Warden. And I'm sorry about your telephone.' She was used to him, his prim ways were touching. She didn't believe he was out to cheat anyone, he was too kind. Loveliness was fond of him. He allowed her to tidy his trestle table, watching her climb like a crab.

'Our residents need watching, guiding. Firm shepherding and example.'

His mouth grimaced again. He'd seen Sylvie shuffling those cards. She pretended it was innocent; all games of chance corrupted. She knew his ruling about sharing, why had she taken a newcomer? They were full.

'He arrived on Christmas Eve. I had left, Cap let him in. He is in need and quite a nice old man. I think Mac and Mr Silk are sufficiently mature to share. They all enjoyed the tree. Did you see Loveliness?'

'Now there is innocence, Sylvie. She must never be corrupted. Our task is indeed responsible.'

'If you'd not gone away you could have joined in. You would have seen how innocent it was. The worst that happened was the phone being broken.' She wasn't afraid of Warden, she pitied him. His telephone was so often abused the Post Office delayed mending it. They weren't a registered charity, they might be cut off for days.

'Sylvie. Sylvie.' He ran a tired hand over his piebald beard. He was weary of ingratitude, of things getting broken. Loveliness was his star, alas under the bad influence of Cap. He'd made her the hideaway under the stairs where she could be at peace. He'd removed bricks from the wall, glassing the space in to give light for her pretty scrapbooks. He liked looking at them himself, they were perfect in their way. Gym tunics were flattering to young and old, she was a darling. His lips moved. 'Loveliness,' he murmured. Loveliness, pride of the house.

'Did you say something, Warden?'

He blinked. He'd been obliged to visit the West Country, he had business ties. Had the newcomer any vices?

'He's lonely! That's not a vice or crime. He talks about wood carving.'

'Be vigilant, observe the rules. Time brings its own reward.'

Warden stared hard at her bust before he returned to his file.

In the kitchen Cap was wrapping Loveliness in a shawl before she put her inside the shopping trolley. They were giggling. The cats jumped at Loveliness's hands as she rubbed a sour puff over her face. She used powder of pinkish grey.

'I'm making Babe cosy. She likes wool near her skin, don't you my tender heart. What's up, Sylvie? Has Warden been making a pass?'

'Warden's not like that. He says I'm not strict enough.'

'Ignore him, you needn't listen. You look as if you've got a hot flush.'

'Don't talk like that.'

'Why not? You say you've got problems with Tim. Make him jealous. Start practising on Warden.'

Loveliness shrieked into her cupped hands. It was so funny. The cat jumped at the puff.

'I'm not blushing or anything, I'm just saying what Warden says, that I'm not strict enough. Have you seen Every this morning? I expect he's lonely.'

'That's his lookout. Warden shouldn't have come back early, spoiling all our fun.'

Cap finished swaddling Loveliness. She opened an old umbrella over the trolley.

When the residents had realized that Warden was watching they'd gone silent. He'd made them feel guilty though they'd not been doing wrong.

He often had that effect, that's why they jeered at his rules. They had each gone off to their rooms; hiding was natural to them.

Each day Sylvie visited them when she got to work, trying to get them to talk. Later she gave reports to Warden for inclusion in his files. There was no sound from Mac and Mr Silk, no praying or thudding of knives. Residents tended to sleep a lot inside their rooms. She knocked again at the dragon-painted door. Every was at the window again, with his back to her. His breathing sounded hoarse.

He turned slowly, showing no recognition. His colour was yellowish, the veins in his eyes were bright.

'How are you today, Every? I've been telling Warden about your wood carving.'

He coughed, covering his mouth. He stared back at the road, as if she hadn't spoken. She was frightened; his breathing was so bad.

Warden was in the kitchen when she went back, talking to Sole. Sole was different. He never stayed long, though he was accepted as permanent. He put down his bed roll anywhere and was rather a cheerful man. They all liked his lumpy face and his habit of cracking his fingers. He was respected for his skill with string. He could make knots and mend items like clothes pegs and clothes lines. He could splice broken wood as well as mend broken pans. He was rarely seen without string in his knuckled hands. He liked cats' cradles. Unlike the tennis table the kitchen table was sturdy. It could seat twelve. Warden dreamt of one day seeing all the residents round it, happy, rosy, hungry, partaking of Sylvie's cooking, having first prayed. Their food was basic owing to lack of cash. Potatoes baked in their skins, porridge with salt, cheese. Sausage and onions made a treat. A local supermarket sometimes allowed them food that outran it's selling date. One week they dined on jam roll, another time hazlenut yoghourt. Sylvie collected residents' rents each week. Those on assistance were reluctant to pay. Fridays were often days of arguments and lies. Loveliness, being a pensioner, thought she should live rent-free. Warden's age and finances weren't known. Sylvie gave advice about sick benefit or application to the job centre; meals remained haphazard. There were no chairs, only orange boxes. There was usually someone in the kitchen waiting to be handed tea. A hot drink in the hand, feet under the table gave you a secure feeling, especially with Warden or Sylvie to listen to your ailments or complaints. It made you feel important. No one liked punctual meal times or grace; Warden lived in hopes. He also hoped that one day they'd keep the house tidy, mended, clean. Loveliness sometimes dried knives as well as dusting his desk. Warden didn't like her playing with Cap, indulging in imaginative foolishness, making a silly noise. He was telling Sole how he felt about self-discipline and etiquette while he sipped his tea. Sole nodded sympathetically. Life was a sober business.

'Warden, I'm afraid Every is ill. His eyes are red, he's dribbling. I'm worried. Will you come?'

Warden asked if the chap was feverish. Chaps used to exposure from the elements went down fast when they came inside. He'd seen it often in the army. Sylvie must take his temperature.

'I can't. I don't know how.'

'Sylvie, Sylvie, I thought you had nursing experience. My my, I'll have to show you won't I? I'll come myself.'

Sole looked at her kindly. He'd no idea what to do with a thermometer either.

Warden was glad to move out of earshot of the two outside playing with cats and umbrellas. Loveliness shouldn't be out. He went to his first aid cupboard. Disinfectants, burn ointments, bandages, a thermometer, nothing in the way of pills because of the weak natures of his people. Surgical spirits, even a stomach powder could lead to trouble, wasn't worth the risk. He'd read of the pitfalls. Mac was his worst anxiety. Sylvie disappointed him, not knowing simple first aid.

'Poor old chap. In much pain are you?' He saw the sandwich boards, proving that the old man worked outside. He saw the three cushions laid in a row making a makeshift mattress. He heard the old man's groans.

'Stick out your elbow. Bones aching? Watch me, Sylvie. Into the armpit with the thermometer. Like this. Better be safe than sorry.'

He spoke of the danger of biting on glass, of children or elderly swallowing poison, the mercury in the glass. He

38

leaned towards her ear as he explained, his beard tickling her cheek. She smelled his vinegary breath. He hissed that the chap was battle-weary, he should know. He had had years of military experience. The chap needed bed rest, hot drinks, the touch of a woman's hand. Later, when he felt stronger, little Loveliness might perhaps sing a song to him (outside his bedroom of course, he didn't believe in residents entering each other's bedrooms. Mixing and sharing was dangerous, the sooner Mac and Mr Silk were reallocated the better.) She might sing something similar to the song she'd sung yesterday. He was fond of a tune called 'Stardust' himself.

'And less drinking my good man.' He turned to Every again. 'I take it you know my rules. No intoxicants, no gambling, no twosomes, not at St Harmony. And I discourage idling.'

Every closed his eyes. First the rag-picker and now Warden Hemm accused him of something he'd never done. It was unjust, he was a sober man.

'Warden, I don't think Every drinks.'

'You are forgetting, I have experience. His symptoms speak louder than words, the chap is his own worst enemy. See, can you spot the mercury? It's high, look closely. Quite a fever.'

He leaned to her again, pricking her cheek with a whisker, pressing up to her bust. He replaced the thermometer cap before she'd been able to see. She hoped he'd not felt her shyness. Was Cap right? Was Warden a letcher or their saviour, or something in between? She rubbed her cheek.

'Sorry my . . . dear. I ought to get my beard trimmed. What? Have I made you sore?'

He touched her face with a dry forefinger. A drop of disinfectant was needed. Adorable . . . quite adorable.

'What do you mean "adorable"? I've never been called that in my life.'

'It's time you were. I mean it, adorable girl. You need

someone to look after you. That person could be me. I have neglected you. I will escort you home later.'

She went silent with surprise. She loved driving in cars. Warden never offered to drive the residents anywhere in his red Ford. His Ford was his pride. He kept it for his trips to the West Country. She'd be his first passenger.

'I'm going to my office now, to write up the chap's file. See you later . . . adorable.'

She fetched Every some tea. She tried to make him drink.

'You must get well, Every. I want you to stay a long time. I want you to join in, carve ornaments. Only I wish you were more comfortable.' His cushions kept slipping apart. He lay stiff-faced. He didn't complain. She put his tea near his hand. He twitched but didn't speak.

It was time to start the evening meal. She'd get it started, Warden and Cap could serve it later. She laid out sausages to prick. There were onions to fry too. She was dying for Warden's red car. The onions made her eyes cry, though she peeled them under the tap. She heard the bump of the shopping trolley again on the step, heard Cap and Loveliness shriek. Loveliness made a face from under the umbrella.

'Intruders. Intruders again. Somebody is spying, Cap.'

She pushed the cats off her shawl, lifting her arms up to Cap.

'Sylvie ain't no intruder, Babe. Here Sylv, take this for your eyes. Any milk left for Loveliness?'

'There were two pints. Somebody took them. There's only enough for tea. Cap, Every is ill. He's feverish, he has to have hot drinks.'

'Loveliness must have her bottle, mustn't you, Babe?'

The more milk they ordered the quicker it went. Cap liked feeding Loveliness her doll's bottle, inventing a world of dolls, speaking in doll's talk. Sylvie didn't check them. Cap was better engaged in dolls' games at home than picking up men in the West End of London.

'He's very sick. Leave some for him, Cap, please.'

'Poor sod. Looking for sympathy probably. I knew he was bad when he come.'

Cap rubbed Loveliness with the powder puff again before putting the bottle to her lips. She'd go under the tree again later. She asked what illness Every had. All that tramping in the streets was enough to make anyone feel rough.

'Exposure, so Warden says. And Warden wants me to go home in his car. He's driving me. The dinner is ready to go in the oven when he gets back.'

'Driving *you*? Stone the crows.'

Cap looked amazed, widening her bulbous eyelids. Sole, still at the kitchen table, cracked his finger-joints sympathetically. He liked Sylvie, he didn't like hearing her teased. Sylvie had listened sympathetically to him, finding him mending jobs and things to be spliced with string. She understood his restlessness that made him move on in the summer months.

'Yes.'

'I told you you needed practice. Get practising on Warden. But keep your knickers on, I don't trust his holy chat.'

Sole spoke slowly. He was a serious man though he smiled often. You listened when Sole spoke. 'Warden is lonely too.'

'Pull the other one, Sole. Warden's a sly old sod.'

'Sole may be right, Cap. Warden has a lot of responsibility. He looks after all of us. Who is responsible for him?' She wanted to feel sorry for him to lessen the nervousness she felt about going home with him. She knew Sole understood.

'He's sly. He dyes his hair. Most probably he wears corsets. I know men, don't forget. Loveliness is peckish, aren't you, Babe. I hope there's afters for dinner.'

'Rice pudding.'

'Rice? Is that all?'

'Not everyone paid rent this week.' Sylvie looked towards Loveliness. How she disliked her sometimes. She looked so insolent, crouching under the golden boughs like a troll. Loveliness was the worst at rent evasion, and had a greedy appetite. She stole milk too. Food didn't stay long enough at St Harmony for them to need a fridge.

'Don't look at Loveliness. We're not rubbish you know, not living on your charity. Just 'cos Warden is driving you home you needn't get ideas. When did you last have a date?'

Apart from Tim, Sylvie had never had a date. She'd listened to Cap and Loveliness talking about men, about love and proposals. Loveliness liked it known that she'd driven men wild in her time, that she was single from choice, that the best life had to offer was feminine and small. She loved playing mothers and children and talking about love. She didn't like the thought of Cap looking after Every with hot drinks, nor would she sing him hymns.

Warden was waiting for Sylvie, buttoning his military coat. His cap was pulled firmly over his nut brown hair. His beard looked freshly combed. Gauntlets poked from his shoulder strap, the tongues of his brogue shoes shone and the knob of his silvery cane. His eyes were bright as he helped her with her old grey coat, his fingers brushed at her bottom. The giggles that came from the direction of the tree didn't stop him poking her with his cane.

'Don't know about you m'dear but I'm a fresh air addict. Hard work, ozone, discipline keep me working. I like a walk about this time of day.'

'I thought we were going by car. What about the red Ford?'

'No no. Shank's mare. A good quick march.'

'Why not the bus? It feels so cold.'

The bus would feel safer. The streets separating home from St Harmony were dark. Warden seemed so excited. She began to regret the arrangement. She wished she had not told Cap.

'No, adorable. Come, step smartly.'

She tried to talk loudly, to distract his touching hands. She spoke about Mr Silk and his meditations, about Every wanting to carve wood. He walked as if he were trying to march, lifting his limping foot, pulling his stomach in. His vinegary breath fanned her cheek.

'What happened, Warden? How did you hurt your leg?'

'Copped it in forty-four. Shrapnel. I was a Major y'know.'

'I didn't know. What did you do after that?'

'Various positions. Never lacked employment. Not like our dear ... wanderers. Authority comes naturally. I taught. Girls' school in South London.'

'What happened? Why did you leave? What happened to the school?'

'Closed down. Headmistress a cripple after a fairground accident. She married into the church later, so I believe. I'm proud, Sylvie, of St Harmony. I trust my staff. We'll win.'

'Staff? But there is only me.'

'I mean you dear ... Adorable.'

'Cap helps of course. She helps a lot, she's fairly reliable.'

'Don't mention Catherine Jones. Dirty. A bad influence on Miss Loveliness. But you, Sylvie, you shine. You are ... adorable.'

He paused, his breath coming in gasps. He leaned against a post, touching her harder.

'Don't, Warden. Please don't do that.'

'We have worked in harness for some time. I shouldn't have neglected you, I've been remiss. I'm remedying that state of affairs.'

'No, Warden.'

'Why not? Give me your ... M'dear, we must get acquainted.'

'Your beard hurts. Stop. Look, Warden, that is my street, the second on the left.'

'I know. I know. Naughty little filly, I'll see you to your

gate. I know more about you than you surmise. Your spouse paints don't he? And you, Sylvie, are, shall we say, frustrated? Just a shade one way and another.'

'No. What are you saying. Stop, Warden.'

'I think . . . yes. Dark little horse. Adorable.'

'Warden, I lead a quiet life. I'm not used to this. I like working at St Harmony, don't spoil it. No.'

'Come. Just a peck, give me your mouth. Afraid of the jealous hubby?'

Behind her was the Community, ahead was Tim, bored with her, bored with his home. She'd never felt a beard before, or felt such shaky lips. They were wet, his nose poked like a snout, his vinegary breath rasped. Lonely Warden was soaking her with his brown and white whiskers. She longed to be safe at home or at the Community. The red Ford or a bus would have been safer. Tim had never stuffed cold fingers inside her coat, or kneaded her bottom with his hands. Was this what Cap meant by 'practice'? He'd lost his military bearing, was grunting unpleasantly.

'That's enough. You're rough.'

'No, no. I know when to halt. I am experienced, dark horse, in love as well as battle.'

'I'm not like that. I am afraid.'

'Of whom? Of me? Of hubby seeing? Leave it to me and in the fullness of time, yes. Yes, Sylvie, you must move in with us.'

'Move in? You're behaving like an animal. You're too old. Don't.'

His choking was like a bark. He drew his stomach in again, wiping his beard dry. He turned, walking the way they had come. His cane tapped unevenly. He didn't wave at the corner but pulled down his cap and went. She settled her coat again walking towards her gate. It hadn't been kind to mention his age or call him an animal. Poor Warden. She went in.

'What is the exuse this time? This lateness is becoming a

44

habit, Sylvie.'

'I would have telephoned, Tim. The phone is broken
again. The newcomer Every is ill.'

'You put *him* before me? You give all your energy to
those failures? I'm mystified. Imagine buying *them* a tree.'

'I did give you something, Tim. You hate Christmas,
you always have. The residents loved the tree yesterday and
had a lovely time. If you ask me you're jealous. Is your
painting not going well? Is that it?'

'Why do you ask? You're not interested nor have you
ever cared.'

'Do you care about my work? I'm tired, Tim. Now I
want some peace.'

'Tired? Peace? *I'm* tired. I've something to be tired about.
I've been working all day, not like you, you only waste
your time with that lot. Why don't you go and live with
them?'

'As a matter of fact I might. Sombody has to earn money.
You don't earn anything, I must. I might go to them and
stay.'

'Do. Do.'

He turned a flat pained look on her. He looked as if she
sickened him. He didn't need her. They did.

✷ Five

Tim cursed his own hastiness. He'd not meant Sylvie to take him literally. He'd not meant that she should stay in that silly place, he'd just wanted to frighten her into giving him more attention. It wasn't that he didn't want her, he just wanted her different. Why couldn't she stay as she had been when they'd first met, all meek like Sister Cecilia. He blamed that place for the change in her. She'd got above herself, anwering him back, all uppity.

He threw a quantity of paint over the dark dog he was working on while he considered Sylvie's shortcomings. He'd been hasty because of being angry. The irony of it was that he scarcely noticed if she was home or not unless he felt hungry. The sight of her face, red as mincemeat reminded him of his tea. Bold creature, how selfish she was, not caring twopence about his work. He'd been fair and square from the start. 'I'm Irish and I paint,' he'd said. She knew how he felt about work. He believed that laziness corrupted, hard work won the prize. He'd told her about his family back in the old country, about his father, mother and his granny. There had been uncles and aunts too, so he believed. Alas, he couldn't remember one of these good persons, he'd been so long away. His faith had lapsed as well. He still put his Mam and aunts on pedestals, good lovely women, why couldn't Sylvie be like them? It must have been his background that formed his dislike of greed, inadequacy and sloth. Why hadn't Sylvie stayed like Sister Cecilia who first taught him to paint? He'd seen her, thought of Sister. 'I'm Irish and I paint.' Only her thick clothes, her weight, her pitted skin concealed a weak character. She'd wanted to marry quickly, her idea, not his. She'd been training in some class of secretary work, he'd never found out what. The day came when she won a considerable amount with a pools coupon, though she'd known he disliked gambling. It had seemed prudent to accept the cash. She wanted to purchase a house, he'd said the one they were renting did well enough. With cash in hand he was freed of outside employment, free to paint full time. Naturally she made over the money to him, as any wife would. For formality he'd protested, inwardly his heart sang praises. Own boss at last, cash in the bank, real freedom. She'd changed then radically. His shining dream of a helpmeet had soured. She complained of the furnishings in the home, she wanted to waste his money. He saw no point in spoiling her with modern gadgetries, the money must last. Women were better kept busy. The money might have been ill-gotten, no one could fault his handling of it. He only asked to be allowed to paint, to develop his brave talent. He changed his style, he abandoned his early painting-by-number kits, he tried water colours. He tried copying. He discovered the splash and throw approach. His sensitive nature was best suited to hurling paint, attacking his canvas at speed by using various tools. His brown and black paint settled naturally into the shape of dogs. He did toy with rats and porcupines, but he preferred dogs. Recently he'd taken to laying his canvas on the floor, throwing himself onto it, getting quite marvellous results. He used a bike wheel too and sometimes Sylvie's mop. The fly in the ointment was Sylvie. She grumbled. She complained of paint everywhere, of the state of his painty clothes. One day she slipped in some paint, hurting her foot. She'd gone out and taken that job. He'd not believed she'd hurt her foot. He had objected. He said that he needed her, She'd been uppity then, accusing him of hiding from life. It was *she* who hid from life, accepting work with that charitable nonsense by the name of Harmony, run by an eccentric named Hemm. She had intentionally obstructed him, directing her energy that should be kept for him towards a lost cause. Home fires were neglected in favour of outside lunacy. He'd been patient, never unreasonable. Prices had risen she'd said, she needed more money. True, true, but why at that job? Why there? What had Harmony got that he hadn't? Why couldn't she market his work? He blessed his sense in appropriating the cash, had he not done so she might have been tempted to make it over to Hemm for his vagrants and tramps. Since that time she had become less humble, more uppity, a bold creaure, wanting to 'talk things out', a deplorable habit. He wanted to talk about art, his art especially; she had no time for that.

Well now, he wouldn't plead, let her join them for good, live in. He'd have peace without her. Peace and paint and time. How glad he was now that he'd not told her of the time he'd tried to sell his paintings. His copyings of Mohammed Ali, the Wombles and President Nixon were ahead of their time. He'd met with apathy. She'd never know about that office boy shouting, 'Another Picasso outside, shall I tell him where to put his work?' Swine didn't appreciate pearls, that was the moral. He struggled on, perfecting his random method, splashing, throwing, hurling, wheeling and falling on paint. An hour or so of such work left him calm and sleepy. He ought to pity Sylvie, anyone could scrub, mop up after destitutes. The artist dealt with truth. A person lacking insight, soul was tragic. No wonder he preferred painting dogs to people. One day his dogs would grace a public building. In time, in time, no use forcing results. He'd be better with her out of the way, he wouldn't be lonely at all. He could still hear her words, 'Someone must earn, you won't so I must.' The creature. Her spots, her wrongly buttoned coat, her hair all gave him the heaves. To think that once he'd even thought of her as Rubenesque. She was moving about overhead, stamping her feet, packing things probably. Let her. Peace and the time to paint. She was coming down now.

'Tim, did you mean it about me living at St Harmony?'

'It's up to yourself. I evidently don't satisfy you. Your own home counts for nought. You come in quite late, night after night. I evidently mean less than that place.'

'I couldn't help it. Warden walked me home.'

'Oh did he indeed? And what has he in mind?' More to the point what had Sylvie in her mind? She had a suggestive mind, a mind full of dirty ideas. He'd not forgot her wanting to drink brandy with him in bed. On Christmas Day of all days. She knew his views on liquour. He'd tried to humour her, pouring brandy over the pudding because of her silly eye. Let her go, let her join her own level with that company of dwarfs, tramps, drop-outs. All in all he'd seen few sunny days since leaving Sister Cecilia. That Hemm was responsible for a pack of misery. He was responsible for himself. And if not he then who? Without that creature to hamper him he'd have time for intellectual pursuits, radio talks, matters above her head. He'd read as well. He sighed so loudly it sounded like a howl.

'I'll tell Warden that I'm moving in. He'll be glad of more help.'

'I've no doubt he will. No doubt at all. I thought you said they were overcrowded.'

'Room can be made. It's urgent.'

'May I as your husband ask where?'

'Look, Tim, I asked you if I could go. Some wives wouldn't, they'd just leave. They need somebody night and day. Warden is overworked. Until Every is well I will stay. It's my duty.'

'Duty? From you, Sylvie, that is rich. Ha ha.'

'I'll be back on Saturday to cook. And buy the groceries.

All right?'

'I understand. Weekly boarder. That's grand, girl, you go. You go.'

He knew Sylvie. She was excited, her voice gave her feelings away. You'd think she was off on holiday instead of going to work overtime in a doss house. He wondered how much she had packed. Which nightie was she taking? *He* didn't care, let her go. Let the freak join the freaks, give him peace.

'Saturday will be here soon. You'll see Tim, time will pass fast.'

'I'm not worrying about my time. *I* have work to occupy myself with. You go, girl, go now.' He'd sleep all the better without her snores in the other bed. She'd slept like a dog even on their wedding night. As a gentleman of sensitivity, not to say shyness, he wouldn't, he couldn't have disturbed her. He'd been considerate of her ever since. A mercy they had no youngsters, they might have developed like her. He'd possibly miss her cooking, such as it was. Other things would more than compensate. He'd read, he'd paint, he'd think. *She* never touched a book, they lived on separate planes. This was the best thing that had happened since that win on the pools.

'I'll cook you something first. What would you like to eat?'

'Pray don't concern yourself. Go off and cook for that lot. They need you, remember?' Make her feel guilty and failed. she deserved a bad conscience. She deserved nightmares.

'Don't take that attitude.'

'What attitude do you expect, girl? You've given me quite a raw deal.'

'I made over the money to you. That win on the pools. You left your job you never bought a home.'

'That's right, drag that up. You only did as any wife should. To hear you it might be the crown jewels you gave up. You've lived comfortably. Cook or not, as you please.'

50

He would have bought a house had it been advisable. She was intolerable.

'I'd like us to part friends. Until Saturday. It is Christmas, after all.'

'You would? I see. How much has Christmas to do with it and how much has Hemm? How does *he* fit into the picture?'

'Warden? He is a gentleman. what are you inferring?'

Tim didn't imagine it this time. Her colour was redder, her lip and nose glistened. so Hemm was behind this. He remarked quietly that if Hemm was a gent he'd have no time for her.

'You're getting the wrong idea, Tim. I think Warden will move upstairs. He'll leave his room free so that I can be near Every to nurse him.'

'I see, I see. You're all settled and suited then. I'm relieved, girl.'

'Don't be sarcastic. They need me. Warden is worn out.'

'With what may I ask? Doing what?'

'He drains himself, he works for others' good. He doesn't hide away dreaming like some people.'

'Meaning me I dare say? From my own wife that's charming.'

'I didn't say you. If the cap fits wear it. I'm going. I'm taking my holdall. I've packed.'

Tim ate a lonely tea of toast and marmalade. He tried to stop wondering about Hemm's bed. Tried to stop imagining her hair on his pillow. She'd be switching his bedside lamp, wiping her nose on his tissues. What were his intentions? The Sylvie he knew was gone. Bold creature, let her go. He picked up his brushes, flung them down. He couldn't settle. He got his bicycle, riding in short bursts from wall to wall across his dog canvas. The paint squelched under the wheels, making a slithering sound. 'Syl-vee. Sylv-ee.'

℥ Six

On Saturday when she came back she'd changed still more. She didn't glance in his direction but walked into the kitchen to put her shopping down. He had been forced to leave his canvas, go to her, ask if she was making elevenses. She'd barely answered. She was going back to the super-market for more groceries. For the rest of the day she shopped, cooked, scrubbed out the kitchen with an aloof face. By Sunday night he was longing to know what she'd been doing at that place and what had been going on. He wanted to tell her about his own work, about the play he'd heard, how he'd listened to the news. Her remark about hiding from life rankled. He'd listened to topical events, had learned of wars, political movements, commercial enterprises and been quite surprised. He'd not realized that the world was in such a state of struggle. In the north of Ireland, his birthplace, it was quite shocking. He'd listened to show Sylvie he could. The play had been incomprehen-sible, likewise an interview with a painter, though the fellow seemed to do well enough, selling his work. He wanted to ask her if she knew his name. The sight of her enraged him all over again, he loathed her fat lips. She'd cooked non-stop without a word being said. She'd risen early on Sunday to continue chopping, stirring, rolling dough in a way he'd never noticed before. Chagrin gave way to impatience, he wanted her out of the house so that he could peep at what she'd made. The fridge was crammed with cooking. The tasty smells tickled his palate, his stomach rolled.

'Why did you make so much? You know I eat almost nothing,' he said, as she put on her coat.

'I've prepared your food for the week. You need only heat up the dishes, there's nothing for you to do. Goodbye till next Saturday.'

The front door banged. He felt his eyebrows twitch with irritation. She cared nought for him and his welfare. The house was quiet as death. He might as well see what she'd concocted. A poor kind she'd turned out, and him a man of talent. Pies, cold meats in aspic, puddings and salads met his eyes. There were jellies and trifles as well. He reached out a starving hand. Hmph. For an indifferent cook she'd not done badly, and about time too. Obviously this activity at the cooker was the proof of her bad conscience; she was saying sorry by means of home-cooked food. He bit into a pie. Not bad, not bad at all. A bit of kidney made a welcome change. He tried another, mollified. Inside the third was an egg, hidden in veal and ham. He switched off the radio, he'd no appetite for solemn sentiments, he was deeply concerned with the pie. The golden centre, the egg white surrounded by meat in a rich pastry was lip-smacking. She'd dated each dish to avoid anything going stale. This pie was for Friday, 'Grosvenor' was its name. He'd heard about these pies. This one hit the spot, soothing the turmoil caused by his creature of a wife. He licked the crumbs from his fingers.

Later, on his way to the sweet shop, he passed the electric shop with the televisions that winked in the window. Of course, that's where he'd noticed them, there was a Grosvenor now, being nibbled by a child. He watched, tasting each bite, his lips copying the child. Until now he'd refused to own a set, a pastime for barbarians and those like his wife, of inferior and simple mind. He deserved a change. Why not? She'd got *her* change. His turn now, he'd buy a small

53

television, watch a little, refresh and recharge his mind. Naturally he would only watch culture programmes, designed for intellectuals, artists, thinkers. Next morning he had a serious talk with the man in the shop, making his needs clear. He picked the cheapest, thrifty as always, no extreme actions for him. The man understood, recognizing a better type of customer, one with an eye for quality. He demonstrated the switches, explaining the various channels. He'd deliver it that night. He winked then at Tim. Nothing like the company of a good television when you were grass-widowed. Tim frowned again. How did the fellow know?

So the set was installed by Sylvie's chair in the back room. That night was a red letter one, Tim was in his glory. He selected his supper first. With lips and tongue working at his meal he settled for his first night's viewing. He watched the artist who he'd heard on the radio last week. He admired his eyebrows neat as stitching above rather soulful eyes. He'd tidy his own brows one day, when his turn came to be viewed by millions. Though it was possible he might refuse to expose himself to *hoi polloi* who might not understand his art. His dogs were unique. He would decide when the time arrived, meanwhile it was time to rest. He needed feeding up. He fetched more pie from the fridge. He marked the programmes sufficiently erudite for his eyes and ears in the *Radio Times* and watched the clock impatiently. Within two days he was in love with his set, viewing from dawn until close down. When there was no programme he watched the empty screen. He shut the front room, he'd take a total rest from paint, from dogs, from toil. His new look-and-listen hobby was activity enough, he'd give it all his strength. He'd say nought to Sylvie about it, not that she'd care anyway. He watched, he ate, he slept, his mind in a dozy haze. He forgot Sylvie, his set was a fresh new joy. Viewing and food and sitting gave him fresh vigour and strength. He felt it might even be possible to save his marriage, what little was left of it.

Next Saturday was the same, no greeting from her, not a hulloa. She boiled, she moiled until late the next day. He longed to ask her how that place was getting along, if the old man was any better, and above all about the sleeping arrangements. What had she been doing, the creature? She had a bad look in her eye. Not that he was jealous, only curious. Well, two could play at games of silence, he had *his* secret now, his set that he'd hidden away in the shed. He pictured her surprise if she knew of his happy week, his eating and viewing while wedged into her armchair. He would have liked to have asked her to make a little more than she'd left in the fridge last week, especially that pie, only he wouldn't give her the satisfaction of knowing she'd cooked well. Nothing was more pleasant than feeding his stomach while feeding his cerebral needs. Some programmes made him drowsy, the later more esoteric ones; sleep was as good as learning. Another blissful week passed. Sylvie came, she cooked, she left. He waited to get to the fridge to see what was there before he retrieved his magic lantern from the shed outside. He trembled with joy as he put it in its place by Sylvie's chair. His finger slipped as he switched the knob, tuning to the wrong channel. A new world, a world of commercial viewing met his delighted gaze, a world more fascinating than Aladdin's cave. He gaped. He'd not seen mention of these advertisements in the paper, nothing to indicate that every quarter of an hour he could watch sausages laughing, jelly babies singing, baked beans waging war or a biscuit expressing an opinion. Though of course he *had* seen that Grosvenor pie in the man's shop window, a foretaste of joy. Every commodity necessary to life at home and abroad was handled charmingly. The advertisements were produced with taste and delicacy. The eatable ones were best. He soon picked up the slogans, mouthing them as he watched, singing the jingles as the pictures moved on the screen. He required nothing else.

Overnight he became a commercial addict, turning the sound down after the commercial breaks, refusing the distraction of plays, talks, dancing shows or news. He leaned back in Sylvie's chair while the pretty child touched the bubbles, or the shampoo spoke to the girl. He almost clapped when fish fingers learned to read. This new dimensional world gave him a new lease of life. At close down after the last jingle he went upstairs to dream of commercials. But for his finger slipping he might have missed this enlightenment, the thought was sobering. He plundered the fridge, laying food round the chair as well as on top of the set.

On his return from the sweetshop the electrical man stepped from his door.

'Satisfied with the set, Sir?'

'More than satisfied thanks. A great way to relax after work.'

'Using it a lot then? You should have a colour set, especially for them art shows. The black and whites don't do justice. Look, see for yourself.'

'I hadn't considered . . .'

The man pointed to the sets on his left. Tim saw some crisps whispering secrets. He saw a Grosvenor pie being cut by a man with thick eyebrows. He was convinced then of his course.

'You did say you watched culture shows didn't you? You're missing a bit then.'

'You're right. Silly of me not to have thought.'

It was time he spoiled himself after a lifetime's unselfishness. Sylvie indulged herself. Time for his turn now. It cost a lot, he was guided by the man. Only the best for the customer with an eye for quality. The licence was more as well. It would be larger, heavier to carry to the shed on Friday, a small price for the joys of commercials in colour. Those lovely radiant hues, those heavenly cakes, those sausages,

those slimline laughing chocs quite dazzled him. He liked
the brightness knob, it was a new toy making reds, blues,
yellows stronger and prettier. He squashed snugly into
Sylvie's chair. His set outdid any wife, it pleased, it
soothed, it didn't answer back. It was tragic to have to hide
such spiritual food away on Friday, but he needed her home
to cook. She mustn't find his secret, she might jeer or want
to touch it herself. Nearly a month had passed without her
telling him anything about that Harmony place or what she
was doing there. He didn't care, he had his secret, his community of sweets and pies. Hemm couldn't hurt him now.
Let Sylvie frequent his official bed, let that old man die, let
that gypsy girl go putting paint in people's eyes as long as
Sylvie cooked and left him with his commercials.

When she came in he happened to glance at her sideways.
She was slimmer. Her spots were less red. She'd never been
very attractive, she looked more youthful now. Perhaps she
was eating less. She pounded her pastry as usual.

'I'll be home on Friday next week. I'll go back on Saturday instead of Sunday.'

'You might have let me know, Sylvie.'

'I am letting you know. I'm telling you. I'll be here on
Friday night. Anyone would think you had a woman somewhere. Don't you feel happier now? You look happier.'

He stared. Poor female, she had no idea. She hadn't an
inkling that what he had in his shed outclassed any woman.
He detected a coarsening in her manners, a slummy sort of
approach that hadn't been there before. Not surprising con-
sidering the class she was consorting with. It didn't matter,
their new regime suited them both. She was well matched
with those brutes at Harmony.

'I take it, Sylvie, that *you* are happier. You have that
Hemm all week. I'm fending well enough, I've had to learn
haven't I? Leave on Saturday or Sunday, please yourself.'
He wouldn't mind some Saturday viewing, a pleasure so far
denied. What mattered the most was her food.

'I come home each weekend, at some inconvenience I might add. Perhaps you'd prefer me to stay away altogether?'

'I didn't say so.'

'You're hiding something. What?'

'*I'm* not the secretive one, Sylvie, nor have I complained.'

With his improved appetite she wasn't leaving him enough. Five days rations lasted him two. By Wednesday his fridge was bare, without pie, trifle or snack. For maximum viewing satisfaction he needed a full packed mouth. He'd starve if she left altogether. He wanted no return to the drab fare when she'd lived at home. She mustn't discover his set, or the fact that he'd ceased painting temporarily. To fool her he went to the front room to fiddle with a paint rag. He whistled a Christmassy tune. He'd started a new canvas, he said, she mustn't look at it yet. He waited for the sound of the front door banging behind her. He celebrated her departure by partaking of a whole leg of lamb, followed by two eggy pies. His set was friend, lover, household pet rolled into one colourful package. A week of viewing and no Sylvie was better than a luxury cruise. Later in bed he pondered how much he really needed her. How bad was it between them? *Could* he manage alone? Best not fret, live in the present. He would eat, rest and view.

The day came when he'd eaten the entire contents of the fridge in a night. Glutted, remorseful, he wondered how it had happened. He'd no dog to blame, no one had broken in, he'd not had a blackout. Could Sylvie have cheated, cooked him less than usual? He couldn't exist on sweets alone, the sweetshop lady stared already because he bought a lot. There was no help for it, he'd have to shop at the supermarket. He'd never shopped for groceries before. He remembered her saying that the manager there was kind, letting Harmony have stale items. He might see her there chatting to him or choosing supper for those brutes. He could ask her if she'd stolen any of *his* food to put before Hemm's lot.

He could check what they ate, if they ate better than he. It was strange that she'd lost weight. He might spot Hemm himself. He sighed again, almost choking. He buttoned his overcoat. The middle button broke. He noticed his collars were pinching, his waistbands were rather tight, her poor washing most likely or perhaps he was gaining weight. No harm in winter time. A little more flesh suited him, her being at home had made him thin with vexation, his weight was stabilizing now. She wouldn't notice if he burst out of his skin, the creature.

He rustled a plastic bag, whistling to keep cheerful. He pushed the swing doors of the supermarket, he'd make for the cooked meats first. He looked for a sign saying 'pies'. Surely they sold pies with egg in them? He heard a polite cough. Mr Silk stood near, raising his hat respectfully, smiling his gold-edged teeth.

'Sir Tim. Good health.'

Tim flushed. He liked the 'sir'. He'd met Mr Silk once, the only one to impress him at all. The fellow had manners, a legacy from some oriental shore no doubt. He could find out what that lot were eating for dinner. The fellow had remarkable eyes, you didn't expect blue in an eastern face. He liked the way he clasped his cotton gloves over his chest in greeting.

'Grand thanks, Mr Silk.' He clasped his own hands together. He knew how to adapt to others' customs.

'Shopping for home, Sir?'

'The wife is with Hemm all week, as you know. I'm having to fend as I can.' He sighed with pathos, squinting his eyes long-sufferingly.

'I shop now for Miss Sylvie.'

'And I for myself. Just snacks you know. My appetite is poor. My wife has little time for her old man now.'

Mr Silk looked sorry. He shifted his blue gaze to a pile of brown rice packets. Tim looked back at the meats. How did you cook a sausage?

'What meats do you prefer, Silk? What are you buying for dinner?'

'Meat? Flesh of beast? Not me, Sir. Vegetarian. Better for bodee and mind.' That Tim could imagine he'd touch a finger to dead flesh made Mr Silk shudder.

'Of course. I do agree. I favour the simple life myself. I was just speculating. No meat, naturally. Frugality strengthens the soul.'

'Very.' Mr Silk lowered his chin. He'd come to buy vegetables for Miss Sylvie. The brown rice looked tempting. Secretly he had a longing to taste meat, to touch once-living flesh with his tongue. The Bisto gravy Miss used that time at Christmas with the sausages had smelled so good. He'd stood in the hall and sniffed. He wouldn't like Sir Tim to think he had base tastes. Poor Sir, abandoned by his wife. He too knew sorry times.

'Coffee, Sir? At caff? Please to come with.'

'Er . . . I don't mind, Silk. Yes, why not?'

'Honoured. Very.'

Tim stocked up with saveloys. The plump man and the short oriental stepped towards the swing doors again. Before leaving both purchased bags of King Edwards. Tim filled his plastic bag with crisps, assorted sweets and a prodigious cake.

'Cake with coffee, Sir?'

'No, not if you don't mind, Silk. No snacks between my meals, particularly cake. I'm a bit of an ascetic myself.' Tim looked longingly towards the cake trolley. His mouth had been empty for over half an hour, the longest since Sylvie had deserted him. He didn't want to offend the fellow. 'Er . . . just a small one then, if you insist. A fancy.'

'Sweet food seals friendship,' Mr Silk smiled, choosing a thin biscuit for himself. A natural host, he waited to feed Sir Tim, to compensate for his wifeless state. He shivered in his thin cotton.

'What foods do you enjoy most? Apart from potatoes and

oat cake?' Tim asked him timidly. Silk made him feel gross, a panderer to the flesh.

Mr Silk swallowed a crumb. He explained that a portion of rice, some yoghourt, a handful of vegetables met his daily need. An oat biscuit made a treat. A solitary by nature, he meditated, was beholden to none. Miss Sylvie trusted him, he never owed the rent. He crumbled his biscuit shyly. He didn't condemn those who indulged in meat or sickly foods. He waited for Tim to ask about his room. He'd felt great pain on relinquishing it. His pain and patience had been rewarded.

'I agree, Silk. I rarely taste sugar myself. Or meat or pastry. Now, how are . . . things? I gather there was some bother over sleeping arrangements, some trouble with a cat?'

'Trouble gone. Mac good friend now. No problem. End of subject.' Mr Silk asked if Tim had a faith.

'Faith? To move a mountain when necessary. Ha ha. In point of fact I've lapsed. I'm Irish you know. I paint.'

Tim took a third cake without being pressed. He knew Silk would wish it. He waved his plump hands as he spoke about his dog paintings, of how he was resting now, how television commercials interested him, a field he might enter one day.

'No television at Community. Peace instead.'

'I dare say. Some of us like moving with the times. How is . . . how are everyone else at your place? What are *they* eating today?'

'Busee. Community happy. Every recovering from illness. Mac plays with knives alone.'

'Alone? And er . . . the dwarf?'

'Miss Marker stick to quarters. Fond of scrapbook.'

'I know, I know. Not quite in my line, a bit different. And er . . . Hemm?' At last he had uttered the sickening name of Hemm.

'Sir Warden snug again.'

'But where? Snug *where*? What are the sleeping arrangements?'

'Attic for Warden. Attic is office now. Warden on mattress above.'

Tim released his breath, biting deeply into a vanilla slice. And er . . . who was in the old office where the telephone was?

'Every. Miss Sylvie in Warden's old room through office, in his official bed. I have own room back again, dragon room mine for keeps. No problem. Have a cake.'

Mr Silk leaned back, he'd told the important news. His rage over the knives had been forgiven and forgotten. Mac had forgotten the cat episode. He'd settled back in his dragon room, his mats were in place again, his wall-hangings restored, his nice utensils in their old terrain. There was no more problem with knives. He laughed with relief at Tim. He'd found a friend, he liked him quite a lot.

They left the caff with stomachs gentled and soothed, potatoes in their hands. Tim's heart eased when he heard that Hemm was safe up in the attic, away from Sylvie and her menopausal notions. She'd get little chance of living out her brandy-in-bed fantasies with that sick old man between her and the hall. He asked Silk again, checking that the bed was indeed filled by Every and not Hemm. It sounded safe. He didn't grudge the old fellow her proximity, poor old tramp. Though what use she'd be in a case of real illness Tim couldn't judge. Good old Sylvie, she had her uses, she must have a heart in her somewhere to bother with such sickly nuisances. He felt a great warmth towards Silk, who had given him peace of mind. Relief made him feel quite faint. He still hadn't found out what they ate. He wouldn't mind some egg pie now, followed by pudding and crisps. They parted the best of pals.

Tim went back to prepare his tray, adding a slab of uncooked jelly. He'd pop out later for some chockie bars in case of a need in bed. He felt reasonably sure that Sylvie would tire of the novelty of living in on week nights. She'd come back gladly, having improved her nursing skills. He'd better make hay while he could, feeding and resting and viewing. He felt generous towards the world. He'd buy her a gift of some kind, buy something for that place. Or he might donate one of his canvases for their miserable kitchen wall.

In the morning there was a letter with an Irish postmark. The sender's name and address on the back read 'Your Cousin Phelim, c/o Hillside Bar'. The town was a small one in the northern part of Ireland.

❧ Seven

'What exactly do you want with Warden. He's tired. I don't want him upset.'

'I tell you I must see Hemm.'

The world had changed for the second time. First Tim had discovered the commercial world of television. Now it seemed he was rich. His Cousin Phelim informed him that he was about to come into an inheritance. He'd never give way to Sylvie again, her earnings were unimportant. He was wealthy, he was the boss. She must return. She *must* cook more food.

'Why do you need to see him? What is so urgent?'

'That, Sylvie, is my affair. You could say that Hemm needs to see me.'

'More secrets? I'm deputy. You'll have to go through me if you must see him. Sorry.'

She seemed to take pleasure in crushing him. She was settling herself into that place too well for his liking. Enough was enough. How much had that gypsy girl to do with it? She could continue her work for a time, he wouldn't forbid that. She must return at nights. Her home was with him. He'd even let her watch his set, as long as he controlled the switches. Since hearing from Cousin Phelim he'd come to a decision. He was ready to switch his career. Either he'd go into pie production, eggy ones in particular, in which he'd need Sylvie's help, or he would produce commercials. He had the cash now, he could choose. Again, he might do both. He felt younger, fitter, wiser. But she must come back to him. He was prepared, if she behaved, to fit her out in mink. He could imagine her demonstrating, revealing her pie-making secrets to a select audience. He could imagine her at a preview or attending an Oscar award with him the winner. These ideas came to him when he read Cousin's letter, informing him of a legacy from a deceased uncle. He'd not thought about the old country for a quarter century. Evidently he'd relatives throughout Ireland. Phelim had had trouble locating him. *He* was the beneficiary. He must get Sylvie home.

'He may be your boss. You forget *I* am your husband.'

'So you keep reminding me. It never used to concern you.'

'We're talking about now. I've changed.'

He felt Cousin P's letter crackle against his left nipple. He had prospects. He would demand an audience with Hemm. He'd slim a little, win the world over, particularly his wife.

'Well I haven't changed. Warden needs a holiday. With him away I won't be home at all.'

'Now Sylvie, Sylvie. What about my food?' He'd not meant to sound greedy. He couldn't bear the thought of not seeing her. It was unendurable.

'Listen, I'm taking over St Harmony while Warden is away. I won't have time for you. I'll leave lists, you'll have to shop yourself. I must say you got through a lot of supplies recently. You can buy cold food or do your own cooking until Warden is back again.'

'I'm coming to see Hemm, I tell you.' His resolve to stay cool mustn't weaken. Was she demented? Silk had quite reassured him in the supermarket. Now doubts returned about Sylvie's feeling for Hemm. She'd got thinner still, and prettier. His heart cried inside, 'Syl-vee.'

'You'll have to book an appointment.'

'I tried to telephone. Their line is out of order again. That old man in the office must have broken it. I mean, he does sleep in the office doesn't he?' No harm in checking again, though he believed Silk, the only one worth twopence. Brutes. Gutter lot.

'Don't be absurd. Every is a gentleman.'

'They're all gentlemen according to you. It's in your interest, Sylvie, as well as the interest of that place that I have a talk with Hemm.'

'My sole interest is their welfare. St Harmony is my life.'

'I have a life as well.' He must stay in control. He'd take no lip from anyone, from Hemm, sick or well, or from her. He would ignore his heart's whispering, he would be tougher than she. He was prepared to donate a sum of money if they didn't want a dog painting, but Sylvie must return. He couldn't say fairer than that. An empty stomach and an empty fridge were too much to endure. The creature had changed his eating habits, a change she'd have to maintain. He was prepared to pamper her, buy clothes for her thinner body, a second television even. She must obey. It was surprising that such a wayward greasy wife had so much power over him still.

'Your life? Look at you.'

Her cruelty made him weak. 'Don't, Sylvie. Stop. Won't you please cook something? A small pie? Some sausages?' He hated the whine in his voice. He was so peckish.

'Nothing doing. Sorry. I've only called in for some sketching paper, crayons and paint and things.'

'Why? What for?'

'I'm starting classes at St Harmony.'

'Art? You? Not with that lot?'

'Yes. Where is that silvery paint? I ordered some with the gold.'

'You can't. You mustn't. You're not experienced.' Not content with leaving him to starve she was insulting him in the most telling way.

'Why not? They want to learn. They have a capacity, a

need for expression, for fulfillment. I don't expect brilliance, I just want to help.'

'You can't, Sylvie. You mustn't.'

'Who are you to say? You don't know them. They want to read, want to learn crafts.'

'Craft? Do they indeed? I know this much about them. I know they're nothing (apart from Silk), nothing. Gutter fodder. Brutes.' His voice choked in his throat. How dared she? His materials. She knew nothing about art. She was insulting him purposely.

'Be careful, Tim. That's strong talk. Let me try to explain.'

Her voice went quiet as she spoke of her plans. Each resident had potential. Every liked woodwork, Sole liked working with string. Mr Silk, an enlightened mystic, might do well at book-keeping. They all enjoyed using paint.

'I see, I see. And just how does Hemm fit in?'

Sylvie looked worried. She confided that Warden had changed. Since she'd taken over his old room he'd gone downhill. He spent days in his attic alone. He had no sense of time, he appeared late for meals looking slipshod. He moved overhead at night, restlessly. He didn't comb his hair or use his nut brown dye. He needed to get away. All this weighed on her. She looked less strained when she stopped explaining.

'And what about the dwarf?'

Her face tightened again. She thought of voice training for Loveliness, that is if she'd co-operate. She was, after all, part of the Community, must be accepted in spite of her faults. If Sylvie could help the others, get them involved, active, she would have achieved much. She was concerned about Mac too, whose hobby was throwing knives. People must be accepted despite their shortcomings. She looked Tim full in the face, she'd speak out now. She couldn't stay at home to watch him turn into a pig. He'd become debased. She'd been disgusted to find those mounds of tin cans, sweet wrappings and boxes hidden behind the bin. It was mortifying, what would the dustmen think?

Tim went scarlet. 'Sylvie. Sylvie, I've been so miserable. Come on back here now. Forget about all the rest.'

She didn't reply. She collected the paints, the drawing equipment. She put the books inside her holdall. Only her eyes looked sad.

He lumbered to the sweetshop, avoiding the electrical man's window. That night he ate faster than ever. He ate from self-disgust, failure and banishment. He ate to keep from ripping his clothes and his hair. He ate because he pined for her. He pined for her eggy pies.

He'd go unannounced to that place.

The shabby building, the broken locks, the neglected floorboards were no surprise to him. He wasn't prepared for Sylvie's shouting face.

'You? Who asked you? You've no business here. Out.'

'I've come to see Hemm, please. Where is he?'

She had paint on her hands, along her hair, more brown paint stuck to her skirt. A buzz of activity came from the kitchen, scraping sounds, rustles of paper. He heard Silk say 'veree'. His nervousness left him. The nerve of her, how dare she set herself up? She couldn't teach a dog to beg for its dinner. He just wished he could warn Silk not to take lessons from a rank amateur. How pitiful that they put trust in a traitor, a turncoat wife. He supposed Hemm was aloft, praying or feeling ill.

'He's better today but he's busy. You can't see him just now. And I must get back to my class.'

From under the stairs he heard giggles, a wheezing male cough. The cupboard door opened. A brown tweed bottom curved out, the heel of a brogue shoe, a flash of silvery cane.

'I say, Hemm, may I see you? Not busy are you? I thought you were poorly.'

'Ha. Sylvie's ever-loving spouse. I have been groggy, I'm

holding my own. Cold out, what?'

'Is it? I wanted a word.'

'Just looking at our young friend's picture books. Fond of the past is Miss Marker.'

'So I understand. It's about . . .'

'Go ahead, Squire. You've heard of Sylvie's plan to exhibit haven't you? She's got all her paints and gubbins. It's only a matter of time.'

'Exhibit? Exhibit what? That's rich I must say.'

'I wouldn't scoff, Squire. Sylvie's our miracle worker. She's got everyone doing something.'

'Me too. Me too. Me too.'

'You too, m'dear. You can show your scrapbooks. I was just . . . editing them. Now, Squire, how can I help?'

'It's more a question of how *I* can help, Hemm. I plan to donate a gift. Something for your charity. My wife does what she can. She's lost weight, it's not a life she's used to. I'm planning to have her back. Before she returns home I'd like you to have something to remember her by. She can still work part-time for a while.'

'Beg pardon, Squire? This is new to me. I need Sylvie, we all do. She's getting her leave in due course, when I return from mine. She can't possibly leave for good. A donation you said?'

'I've come into a legacy. I inherit my Uncle's estate. Not much, mind, but I'll be needing Sylvie now. I thought of a painting perhaps, one of my dog portraits for your kitchen. Or you might like some curtains (second-hand ones wear best) or possibly a group outing.'

'A cultural jaunt you mean? I'd have to consult Sylvie, she's the art expert now. But. Squire, she can't leave, that's out of the question. Our cultural officer is too valuable.'

'She's due a holiday, you said.' He wouldn't whine or beg. He was the exchequer man now.

'She goes when I return from the West Country. I'll call a meeting re your proposal. Our residents like to be consulted, we're democratic here.' Warden's voice deepened with pleasure. Handsome of Squire, particularly when funds were stretched. He'd come at a handy time. He'd be in touch, let him know in the fullness of time.

Later Sylvie accused Tim.

'What's going on? What legacy? You've kept very quiet about this. How much? I felt silly when Warden spoke to me, you might have said something to me.'

'I wanted to surprise you. I heard from my Cousin. I thought of a painting for your little settlement. My dogs may be worth a lot one day. I told Hemm in case he had other ideas. Not cross are you . . . love?'

'Firstly I'm not leaving St Harmony. I don't want a holiday either. What Cousin is this? Cousins are new to me.'

'My Cousin in County Down. Cousin Phelim wrote to me about the inheritance, he's the executor. We could visit him if you wish. It's a good while since I took you away.'

'You never have taken me away. I'm not trekking off to the wilds, not me, I'm too busy. And don't ever come near the Community again. Phelim son of who?'

Tim was silent. The name Phelim, like Harmony and Loveliness, were embarrassing names to say. He'd no notion of how Phelim fitted into the family. There were a lot of them, it was all so long ago. The letter said 'Cousin', that's all he knew or cared. His need for Sylvie had become an ache. No matter what she said about him visiting he must go there again. As instigator he must attend that meeting of Hemm's, he must know what was said.

He dressed for the second visit with care. A pity his clothing was tight. He must play his cards right, get her home and cooking as soon as possible. Grosvenors, pudding, meats would be filling his fridge again soon, and Sylvie, thinner, prettier would be at her rightful post, ready to help with his new enterprise after their holiday together.

His coat wouldn't button at all. Had he got plumper since

the arrival of Cousin P's letter? He remembered the old dress suit in the shed, that once his father had worn. He couldn't remember his father, nor did he wish to, that part of his life was done. He'd kept it all these years, waiting for when it might fit. Where previously it had hung like the skin of a gorilla it touched as if tailor-made. This was a dress occasion, he'd arrive dressed for the part. Pie-king, their benefactor, impressario, he'd give the brutes a treat. He might even give them employment one day. Gutter fodder, muck rakers, they'd never achieve much alone (of course he didn't include Silk). He'd set the gypsy girl to packing his pies in boxes, the dwarf could be made to leap from a cake, ideas jostled his mind as he patted the lapels of the coat which had turned mouldy here and there. Fresh air and a hot sponge would fix that, not that the brutes would notice, with their pinched and sorry eyes. He longed for the day when they'd kneel before him. He put on his woolliest scarf, settling it jauntily. His shoes had got lost among the food wrappings, no matter, slippers were comfier in the cold. With quiet pride he walked the streets, his heart beating Sylvie's name.

She was arranging orange boxes to seat the residents round the tennis table. Warden's briefcase was at the top end. Sylvie's astonishment overcame her anger.

'What are you wearing? You look like a poodle dressed for a funeral.'

He wasn't discountenanced. He looked a man of consequence. Where was Hemm this time? It was nearly eight. In with the dwarf he supposed. Yes, he'd surmised correctly, the door under the stairs creaked. Hemm emerged sheepishly.

'Evening, Hemm. I'll sit at the top shall I? I was fortunate in being able to get here. Let me hand you your briefcase.' Tim wiggled his newly clipped eyebrows at Warden in a pally way, to show he was broadminded, a man of the world too.

Warden didn't smile. He always sat at the top. If no one attended his meetings he sat formally alone. This was an extra-curricular meeting. Sylvie's spouse might be the originator, he wasn't in charge, certainly not. Squire mustn't get too big for his boots, or those slippers he wore today.

'That end, Squire, be so good. Looks well, Sylvie, don't he?'

'I'm so-so. Where are the inmates? I've not got a lot of time, I'm due at another meeting, quite an important function.'

'What function? Where?' Sylvie asked rudely.

'My residents will arrive in time. I pinned an announcement on the bulletin board.'

Warden glanced at his peg board. 'Extra-curricular house meeting to discuss charitable donation. Twenty hundred hours.'

'They may not all have seen it. I think Mr Silk did.'

'He'll pass the word. Good fellow and his rice and gubbins. I have informed Loveliness.'

Warden had whispered the information to his young friend under the stairs hiding with her dolly bottles and pictures. He hoped that Cap and Mac hadn't gone on a scavanging jaunt; he regarded the West End of London with disfavour. He relied on Sylvie to keep them in check, to enforce his rules while he supervised their health, administered finances and kept the files up to date. He touched his briefcase, feeling energized, restored. Sylvie's classes were a masterly stroke. And here came Every now with quill pens for the table, on his feet again and mumbling his toothless mouth.

'In case the committee want to take notes, Warden. I fashioned the pens myself. Shall I sit the other end of the table?'

'No thank you, Every. Sylvie should sit there, she's second in command. Now where is Sole?'

'I saw him splicing a potato peeler.'

'He should take notice of bulletins. Everyone can read that much. We'll start.'

'Wait for me. Wait for me.'

Loveliness beat at her door with hands as sharp as claws. Warden would rather she didn't attend, he wanted her for himself, pure, uncorrupted. He didn't want Squire staring.

Then Mac and Cap arrived. As he had feared, they had been wandering. Mac staggered to his room, not speaking. Cap had had a successful day, she'd found parts of a sewing machine, a wooden spoon and several cracked plastic bowls. She had a lit-up boisterous look. Her tongue pushed a sweet round her mouth, her eyes dared them to question her. Wild-haired, wild-eyed she looked like a gutter angel. She lifted Loveliness, settling her legs round her hip.

'Mac's pissed. He's pissed isn't he?'

'Now, Babe, that's his business. He ain't hurting you.'

Loveliness looked at Tim, fluttering her lashes. She'd like to sit on his knee.

'Excuse lateness please.' Mr Silk settled himself cross-legged on a box, his eyes sparking with interest.

'Residents, I declare the meeting open.'

'You must wait for Sole, Warden. He likes meetings. Sole. So-ole are you upstairs or where?' Cap yelled loudly. Sole mustn't miss this chance of seeing Tim got up like a dog's breakfast. She'd bet no good would come of this meeting. Sylv had a face like a boot. Loveliness oughtn't to flirt.

'Here I am folks. Surprise.' Sole crawled from beneath the tennis table. He'd been splicing the broken leg. He liked pleasing Sylvie. He planned to make hammocks for the residents. He was doubtful about Every's bones swinging horizontally in the air though he'd made a good recovery from his ailment. Every was in excellent shape, he'd no desire to return to sandwich boards. He wanted to make them a crib, or a crucifix if they preferred. He motioned for Sole to sit by him. He couldn't imagine any other life than the one he had at St Harmony.

'Would anyone like a pot of tea? Before the meeting starts?'

'Not now, Every. Thank you. Squire has another function to attend. I declare the meeting open. Officially.'

'And I declare it closed. We're waiting for Every's tea. Mac and I are tired. I fancy a tea first. Mac's parched I'm sure.'

'Pissed. Pissed. Pissed.' Loveliness intoned.

'Shut up, Babe.'

'Cap, what did you do in London?' Sylvie had to stop Cap arguing with Warden. Cap was too insolent. She longed to teach her hem stitching clothes for the residents, stop her West End of London jaunts, stop her petting Loveliness. Cap should be *her* best friend.

'We fancied a bit of fun.'

'Pissed. Pissed.'

'I'll announce the agenda. The motion is . . .'

'Motion? What motion? What do you mean, Lord Muck? Just wait for Mac, let's have a drink of tea.' Cap slapped at Loveliness's sniggering mouth.

'Since I am responsible for you being at this table, it's all through my generosity, I think Hemm should be allowed to explain.'

'"I think Hemm." Listen to you. Who cares what you think? You're only Sylvie's man. From what I hear you make a rotten spouse.'

'Don't Cap. That is uncalled for. Let Tim speak please,' Sylvie said in a shamed voice.

'Residents, residents. Remember the St Harmony rules. I called the meeting, I shall take the chair. I wish to discuss the donation from Sylvie's good man, Tim. Now then, Squire, you tell them about it.'

'My Cousin in County Down has . . .'

'Shut up, here comes the tray. Ta, Every. I'm parched.'

Every carried the tin tray with care. Though no great

lover of kitchen work he had made mint tea for Mr Silk to drink from his eastern cup. At last he felt needed, a useful member of the community. Mac fell from his doorway, knocking the tray to the boards.

'Wash going on now?'

'A meeting about a gift. From Tim here. Crazy ain't it? Sit with me, Mac.' Cap patted the box by her side. She smelled faintly of rose soap mixed with her strong-smelling tennis shoes.

'How mush the bugger giving?'

'Mac's right. How much, Tim, you haven't said yet? Sorry I called you no good. Only . . . well you don't half look loopy in that suit.'

'That's all right, Cap. I thought of something for the house, a painting to inspire your own little attempts. Or . . .'

'Or what? We don't need no paintings. We're making our own you know.'

'What about an outing? A group activity?' Tim eased his thumb in his waistband, looking Cap full in the eye.

'Something like the pictures? Babe might like that.'

'The circus. The circus.'

'We need wood for making and carving. And string for my friend here.'

'Givush a set of knives. Or a booze-up.'

'The wiring is old and worn. Particularly my telephone,' Warden said wistfully. Mr Silk was alone in not making his wants felt. Possessions were less valuable than peace in the heart.

'My Cousin in County Down has been in touch. My Uncle died you see. As soon as I can I'm taking Sylvie there on a visit. I shall tell Cousin about you all.'

'Taking Sylvie? Why not take us? Let's all go if you got the cash. Stone the crows, Tim, all of us need a change.'

'I meant . . . more of a token. Some gift to remember Sylvie.'

'Why? She ain't leaving.'

Warden fingered his beard. They must vote. They must be wise. His voting papers had got soaked with tea. He wrote in his crabbed hand. He read out the choices, asked for a show of hands. A film. A circus trip. Equipment (wood, string, paint, er . . . a dartboard, not knives or beer). A trip further afield, not necessarily to Squire's Cousin.

'I didn't mean . . . I didn't intend.' Tim tried to make himself heard against the chatter and waving hands. He'd had no chance, he hadn't explained. He cursed the greedy band. He wanted to give them a dog, a dog painted on canvas. Couldn't they understand? As usual they'd taken matters into their hands, showing no respect. He was their benefactor, not some cheap ticket salesman.

He cursed his Cousin Phelim for being Irish, cursed his own generous heart. Still, he had intended visiting Cousin. He'd have Sylvie with him, though they'd not be alone.

ঞ Eight

'You can't do it, Tim. It's unkind. The residents aren't used to travel. A channel crossing will upset them. Remember Warden's heart.'

'Hemm seems fit enough to me. He was all right at the meeting. He's playing the old soldier again. Have you any idea of the cost of air travel? I'm paying for seven remember, plus you and myself. The mail boat was good enough for me when I travelled.'

'Twenty-five years back, yes. Times change. And the residents are old, most of them.'

'We might return by air,' Tim said thoughtfully. He anticipated a legacy of several thousand pounds, though it might come in the form of bonds. They'd fly back when the money was through. He wished Sylvie would be grateful, unbend. He was doing everything he could, taking the lot of them when all he wanted was her alone. His dream of walking some Irish lough, sniffing at turf fires with just her was ruined. He must wait, be patient, he'd have his real honeymoon yet. He yearned to recapture the time when she'd been like Sister Cecilia, gentle, approving, malleable. There were such a lot of residents. Sickening to have to drag them across the sea after him.

'Must you scrimp?'

'I couldn't afford it. The money may not be much.' No point in giving her ideas, let her think it was a paltry sum.

He'd keep a silent tongue before she suggested handing the lot over to Hemm or those brutes. Once Uncle's estate was drawn up he could move ahead with his plans. He prayed that they'd change their minds, settle for a film or a dog, but he was out of luck, they were wild about Ireland. He had hoped that Cousin might object to such a crowd but his answer had been overjoyed.

'Am delighted, Timothy, that you haven't lost the faith and that you and your wife are so charitable. Bring as many of your English orphans as you wish. Myself and brother Alphonse (Phonsie as he is known) will do all in our power to make the stay memorable. The lost kiddies don't ask to be abandoned. I assume they are all Catholic. We long to meet your bride. We manage to ignore the present Troubles here with our little bar and our caravans that we rent out in season. Your orphans will enjoy a bit of green. God bring you safe to our shores. Your fond Cousin Phelim. PS We will discuss the estate when we meet.'

Tim stroked the two letters written in green ink. Nice that Cousin was so religious. His vans would do very well to sleep in.

'Writes a good letter doesn't he, Sylvie?' He tried to remember a Cousin or anyone called Phelim or Phonsie. The only clear memory he had of Ireland or anyone in it was his Grannie's cooking. Even the face of Sister Cecilia was faded.

'He sounds like a fanatic. I'm glad you never pray.'

Sylvie deplored the change in Tim. His gluttony since he'd stopped painting hadn't ceased. The television set by her chair had been another shock. Materialistic, greedy, he seemed almost unhinged, babbling about a new business, expecting her to be interested in pies for commercials. She'd answered that idea in one short word. He'd got so fat and sloppy. This new Cousin might bring him to his senses. But Warden shouldn't travel by sea, especially at night. Since the house meeting he seemed thinner, weaker, had actually lost height. He spent more time under the stairs with Loveliness. He hadn't repeated his advances towards herself, she didn't mind, she had a lot to do. Ireland was what they needed, a change, a rest, new faces. With the residents along with her she felt differently about the trip. They knew nothing about Ireland though Every had a friend in Limerick.

'You know I'm a baptized Catholic, I told you about Sister Cecilia. Catholicism is strong in me.' He liked the sentiment, he'd remember to use it again.

'Look, Tim. All right. That was a long time ago. I don't care to look like a nun now. If we do go by sea could we kit out the residents with new clothes? They've nothing to wear, only rags, (except for Mr Silk).'

'Could "we", Sylvie? Don't you mean "I"? The money is mine you know. What about making some clothes? I thought you were teaching them.'

'It takes time. Cap is learning. They want to learn, I told you.'

'If I said yes, would I have charge? You said Hemm ought to rest. I mean, we'd share the responsibility but I must be boss, with your help of course.'

'While we're away I don't see why not. Warden could relax, do nothing. A good idea, Tim. We'll go to the high street to shop. Fit everyone with new clothes.'

'Hemm can bring the shopping party in his car if he likes. Save on bus fares.' Also Tim didn't care to be seen with the residents in daylight in his own district, the brutes looked too eccentric. Another good reason for crossing to Ireland at night.

'I'll tell him. He'd probably be pleased to hand over leadership completely. Between us we'll manage the residents.' Sylvie gave Tim a look of pleasure. They'd go to the store where she'd bought 'Heart of a Rose' soap, the place where she'd lost her knickers. Every would enjoy revisiting his old haunts. Much better go there than the West End where temptation lay for Cap and Mac. The New Year sales weren't over, they'd see them properly dressed. She'd heard of the damp chill of Ireland, she too would like to look her best. Tim had never bought her clothes.

Warden was pleased that Tim was taking over command, he had confidence in Sylvie's spouse. He'd drive the shopping party to the store in his red Ford, Squire could take over then. He filled up the car with water, petrol and oil, humming a military tune. He looked forward to inspecting the military operations in Ireland that featured in the news. Squire was acting handsomely, buying them mufti and gubbins. They'd go across like emissaries of peace.

'I want to sit on your knee.' Loveliness pulled his tweed pocket.

'Not while I'm at the wheel, pet.' He looked at her with love and longing. He'd miss her cubbyhole while they were away. Squire and he saw eye to eye about gambling, alcohol, idling and twosomes. Clothed properly they'd show their friends over the water what real discipline was. The Ford couldn't carry them all, Squire and Sylvie could follow by bus. They'd assemble outside the store.

The Ford arrived first. The residents waited for the bus feeling lost, a little afraid. Every looked up and down the street, he missed the Christmas lights.

'Never mind lights now. Can you see their bus coming?' What they needed was puttees, a short back and sides, *esprit de corps*. Sole had tried to be his own barber, hacking his locks with a knife borrowed from Mac. His little friend was better than a regimental mascot.

Sylvie and Tim got off their bus, reassurance for the residents who felt far from home. Every hoped for some of the slippers still on display in the window. Tim felt for his wallet uneasily.

'I want a swansdown frock,' Loveliness simpered.

'Er . . . why not slacks? Keep those little leggies warm. We must be warm for the night crossing.' Tim would never get used to those twisty legs under the gaiters. He voted for kiddies' trousers with loops to go under the soles. Who did the dwarf think she was, demanding white trimmings and fur? And now look at her, pulling her mouth down, showing those snaggle teeth. Holy God, did she *have* to roll on the pavement in broad daylight, making a show of them all? That din would scare a saint.

'Easy now, easy, she's after taking a fit,' he yelled.

'That's no fit, that's tantrums. Now, Babe, stop that. You don't have to wear no trousers, come on into the shop.'

'White dress. White dress.'

'Yes, yes. We'll see about it.' Tim pushed ahead into the store. He'd offered to lay out his money, no one said 'thank you'. Oh no. The miserable little brute, at it again kicking her heels, screeching.

'Babe, people are staring.'

'White dress. I must have white.' Loveliness pointed a claw finger towards the display of perfume on the counter. She'd got her audience, given them a spectacle to remember, she wanted some 'Heart of a Rose'. Tim opened his wallet. He began to doubt the wisdom of his enterprise.

'Listen, Tim, I'll take Cap and Loveliness. You and Warden go with the men. We'll meet here later.' Sylvie's main worry was Warden. His vinegary breathing was shallow, his lips had a mauvey tinge. His fingers had a dry flaking appearance. He didn't trim his nails.

'Cheer up, Sylvie. Buy yourself some pants. Go on, silly cat.'

'I got some here at Christmas. Do you remember? They fell down in the street.'

'White dress. White dress.'

'Shut up, Babe. You've had enough attention for today.'

Cap helped Sylvie choose white knickers for both of them. They fitted Sylvie now. For Loveliness they picked kiddies' double-knit bloomers.

Tim strode to the mens-wear section, not lingering by

the coats. Under no circumstances must they start fancying coats. Costly purchases were out. He regretted the dwarf's scent. He paused before a tie stand. A tie boosted morale, but most of them didn't have collars. He wished they would stop shivering. He wished they weren't so quiet. Sole was rubbing his knuckles, hoping for string gloves probably.

'I suggest hankies, people.' They had some reduced in the sale. The brutes all sniffed as if they had the flu. He caught Sole using his hand. Mr Silk whispered.

'What's that, Silk? White for peace? Ha ha. Very good, I like that.' He'd get them a hanky apiece. And what about socks for Every? He'd spotted the fellow's shoes. Every shook his head politely, longing for a coat like Tim's. Mac fingered a display of hip flasks, extortionately priced. Warden glanced towards Tim, an uneasy look in his eyes. Tim conferred with him rapidly. Any doubts about their partnership dissolved, they'd work in harness from now on. They would ignore Mac for the present, the change in another country might work magic.

'Look. Wellingtons. Over on that shelf. How practical. I'll buy boots for one and all. Look Mac, look at the boots.' Tim would wear some himself, and some for Sylvie too. He had planned something extravagant for her, a watch or a ring for her left hand, a gesture acknowledging their shared years. He envisaged jewels flashing on the hand that baked the pies. He saw the wink on the hand that twined in his while his other accepted the Oscar. *His* diamonds on *his* wife. She'd feel differently about his plans then. Meanwhile boots would do very well. He heard the ladies coming. He heard the dwarf's voice.

'Is that all you bought, Tim? Hankies and Wellington boots. I knew you were mean. You take the cake you do.'

'Hush, Cap. Don't tease. Tim's doing the best he can. He's taking us all away.' Sylvie had to defend Tim. Something about his face touched her. He really tried to please. He wasn't fond of the residents, he'd come shopping for her sake. He hated spending, he'd never had financial success or any success at all. She was quite curious about his Cousins in Ireland. She pointed towards some caps. Were they balaclavas? They looked like army surplus.

'The very thing for a holiday. Here you lot . . . I mean . . . residents. Warm hats. Try them on.'

He took one himself, poking his jawbone into the dark wool, smiling out through the visor. He wouldn't let them see that Cap had hurt his feelings, or that he'd noticed the dwarf giggling again.

'Advance. Charge. Up guards and at 'em,' he laughed. Capped and booted they were ready to take on the world. Warden tried one on. Silvery tufts of beard prodded the stitching, the drop on his nose was gone. One by one they each pulled on a hat, blinking as they settled the neck pieces. They smiled at each other. Mr Silk's unusually blue gaze met Every's red veined eyeballs. Mac's black pupils looked at Cap. Sole's hazel eyes met Loveliness's green ones. Their laughter was infectious.

'By the right. Quick march,' squeaked Warden giving the final command. The handing-over ceremony was over, let Squire go on from here.

They filed from the store, still smiling, their feet at a cheerful pace. They trusted Tim now. They would abide by Warden's precepts, they wouldn't let St Harmony down.

☙ Nine

Warden was the last up the gangplank. His gammy leg dragged more than usual, as if he were in pain. Tim worried a little, he'd looked forward to discussions with Hemm whose attitude towards weakness was so admirable. Tim took back all he'd said against him. The fellow was stirling, with principles that wouldn't disgrace a field marshall. But now he was combat-weary.

Sylvie and he put him on a bench in a corner of the third-class deck. His helmet had slipped across his nose, his breathing was worse, he didn't care who took his briefcase and cane. Had Tim known he'd turn so poorly he would have reserved him a cabin. The rest were better sitting up within sight of each other, not hidden away in bunks at further expense to himself. The leavetaking of England had been timid, booted, shy. Not one appeared to have travelled before, each one looked petrified. The dwarf (he still couldn't bring himself to utter her name) was more spoiled than ever, insisting on being carried. Every tried to stand erect but he'd spent too many years braced between boards. Mr Silk looked calm, his helmet low over his eyes. Tim looked forward to more talks with Silk as well as with Warden Hemm. He'd like to pick up acquaintance where they'd left off at the caff. It would be pleasant to eat another snack somewhere, just Silk and he. He wondered about the quality of the food at the home of Phelim and Phonsie. He knew the Irish ate well, with bacon, potato cakes, cream.

His granny had baked lovely barmbracks.

The engines hummed, quickened, now they were moving away. He looked at their fellow travellers, labourers mostly, taking a late Christmas break. The labourers stared back. Then they got out a bottle to pass round amongst themselves. He wished Sylvie had packed a thermos, they wouldn't dock until dawn. The bottle made a glugging sound down the labourers' thirsty lips. Mac looked and swallowed. A priest and a few nuns glanced at them before closing their eyes, having prayed for the night first. Tim tried to look pious, tried to remember some prayer as he pulled his coat round him. After all, Catholicism was strong in him. He would have liked a coat like Hemm's, a military one. He must get his money first. His days of wearing coats that wouldn't meet were almost over. How cold, how damp it was. The residents kept their eyes open all night except for Warden Hemm.

At dawn Tim went above to watch the boat docking.

It was a strange return to the land of his birth, the land he no longer remembered. He wished he could remember his granny now, not just the taste of her bread. He'd shortly be a man of means, able to look anyone in the eye. His mission was delicate, he wished the residents looked a little smarter. He was confident that once they met Cousin Phelim they'd laugh and talk again. Their caps evidently gave them confidence, they'd kept them on all night. They weren't the same since they'd left the store, they'd lost their *joi de vivre*. Hemm didn't appear to know what was going on.

Their boots clopped quietly down the gangplank. They moved like sleeping ghosts. Their eyes lacked lustre or any interest in the land over the sea, they kept them directed on their boots. Sole chafed his hands. Tim carried the briefcase for Warden who was last. He moaned a little, leaning on his cane.

A man in green clothing stood apart on the quayside watching the priests and nuns. A sleety rain began. The labourers met up with their relatives, they dispersed with happy grins. When the clergy had gone too the man in green walked over. His suede shoes matched his tie and the feather in his hat. He touched Warden's peeling fingers.

'Timothy? Is it yourself? Welcome back to the old country.'

'*I* am Tim. Here I am, Cousin. That is Warden Hemm. Can this really be Phelim?'

'It is.'

'How are you, Cousin P? This is my wife Sylvie. Delighted to meet you at last.'

'Pleased to meet you, Timothy. Excuse me, but who are these.' Phelim tried to keep his Irish smile. But what had Timothy done to him? Who was this dark-hatted gang? Why had he brought hoodlums? Or were they terrorists? Those two old men might well be gunmen and who was that wee cripple? The one carrying her looked a streel. Where were the innocents Timothy wrote of? He couldn't believe his eyes, he'd heard tell of no Warden. Where were the Catholic orphans? He took off his gold-rimmed glasses, polishing them on his gloves. He approved of the look of Sylvie, a bonny woman there.

'These are the residents of St Harmony. I wrote about them, remember? Pleased to be with you at last, Cousin.'

'These? These aren't the orphans, surely? *These?* My apologies, Sylvie. Pleased to meet you, a thousand welcomes. How do you find Ireland, my dear?'

'I can't say yet, can I? I've only just arrived. The crossing was tiring. We sat up.' Sylvie was disappointed in Tim. Warden shouldn't have sat up, he looked done in. He'd carried economy too far. No one of Warden's age or state of health should be asked to sit on a bench all night. They all looked whacked, no wonder nobody spoke.

'Not much further now. I've come to escort you to Hillside, our bar on the side of our hill. The caravans are clean and waiting. I must confess that I did not expect . . . I . . .

86

we had expected wains.' Phelim wished the hoodlums would speak. Had they no tongues? Didn't they understand plain language? Those hats, those boots, those silly looking eyes had come as a square smack in the face. What would Phonsie think? The two old ones shouldn't be let travel, that is if they were old and not hoaxsters. They appeared scarce able to lift their feet or place their right hands in his. He winced to feel the claw of the wee cripple. No matter, he'd show them the hospitality that Ireland was famed for, the holiday of a lifetime. Much depended on the enterprise, he needed to talk with Timothy. Their arrival had started badly, he'd make up now. They'd be safe with him and Phonsie, they could forget violence and crime. He smiled widely. Timothy's bride met with his liking, the one bright spot in the affair. Here now, this way to the train, this way to green countryside. Still and all, they were a tragic lot.

He watched as each one wedged his or herself into the pullman carriage, eyes still down on their knees, not so much as a peek through the window. He looked at Sylvie, he'd point the various landmarks. He'd like her to notice the city first, the grey buildings ripped about by bombs. He'd like her to understand that it took more than a few soldiers to get his country down. Neither bullets nor burnings took a feather out of them, nor yet tanks, armoured cars. In a minute they'd be out of the built-up area, she'd see real country soon. See there, green fields starting, all lovely in the wet. See the grazing stock and those cottages with their farmyards and fowl running round. You didn't have to look far for church spires either, not in holy Ireland. Pay no mind to the soldiers, listen out for the bells. They'd be tolling for holy Mass soon. Phelim crossed his breast. Nobody answered or looked. He thought Sylvie might have cared. He took out his beads from his pocket. If the hoodlums would look just once at him or out of the window, but they only had eyes for their knees. He'd need strength and tenacity to carry out his plan. Why had they dreamed up such peculiar clothes? Phonsie wouldn't like it. He and his brother prided themselves on manners, they listened when people spoke, they smiled to pass themselves. Their good humour brought business, that and his own sharp mind. The Hillside was the finest meeting place in Down. Locals and soldiery, tourists and trippers met in and out of season. Hillside refused no one as long as they'd money to pay. They never closed their door, they catered for all thirsts. It was to be hoped these gaolbirds wouldn't scare folk away. The one they called Warden looked to be a dying man. The more they stayed hidden away the better for one and all, they'd not be a good advertisement for their bar. They showed no signs of an awareness of the Catholic faith or any other faith. Heathen lot, not noticing church bells, not caring. The only asset in the sorry business seemed to be Timothy's bonny wife.

Sylvie roused herself to ask if he was married.

'Married? I thought I explained, there's just Phonsie and myself. We neither of us are fifty, time enough for marriage. Time enough when we meet somebody as lovely as yourself. I hope you stay a long long time.'

'We planned a few days only,' Tim answered curtly. On no account must his cousin get ideas about Sylvie. Obviously Phelim was easily carried away, like Hemm who had had an eye for her, though you'd not think it to see him now, with no thought in his head but getting his next footstep down.

'If Phelim wants us, why not? We could stay longer, Tim, we aren't tied.' Sylvie felt brighter. First Warden had made advances, now, having lost weight and her acne, here came Phelim with admiration in his face. He wasn't bad looking, his gold glasses and his green clothing were charming in a folksy way. She might break a lot of hearts in Ireland, if Phelim was a sample. Her turn might come yet, she'd get experience. Not that she wanted to upset Tim, but he'd neglected her badly. He didn't answer her suggestion but looked at Phelim's prayer-mad fingers feeling along his beads.

'We're beginning to slow down, Cousin. Is this it? Are we there?'

Phelim stood up, pocketing his beads.

'Come little ones, our journey is complete. Uncle Alphonse is waiting at Hillside. Follow Uncle Phelim.' He had a natural fatherliness. 'Little ones' sounded just right. If only they would smile, the miserable mohawks, he was doing his very best.

'This way,' he added sharply.

The road stretched from the little station to the foot of the hill. The residents spread out singly with Warden hobbling last. The sleet was turning to rain, falling hard, soaking their shoulders, beating into their eyes. Loveliness hid her face in Cap's neck.

'Where are we now, Phelim? This is a mountain. Where is the hotel? How far?' Sylvie wondered if she should put her hand in his arm.

'A step just. It's a bar, Sylvie, and this is our hill, not a mountain. One of the green hills of Erin,' he added in a romantic voice.

'It isn't so green today. And so stony. Rain makes everything grey. Have you got a farm as well?'

'A few fowl. The land here makes hard farming. The bar is our living now. Our caravans do help out in summer. We depend on our bar. We run a friendly house, each man gets a drop of what they want.' Phelim winked at Sylvie. His visitors were worse than an attack of DT's apart from this bonny woman. Whatever could she have seen in Timothy there, pulling a long lip now on account of the rain?

The residents saw the vans before they saw the bar. New, glossy white, the vans stood taller than the roof behind. Thin smoke from the house chimney hung sulphurous in the rain. A few fowl pecked in the wet outside the outhouse. The rain beat on the van's metal roofs. A dog barked somewhere. Phelim lead the way past the vans towards the door of the bar. The door had two halves. A man leaned over the lower half, watching the visitors file in. Fair hair hung in a slab over his eyes. He wore a white jersey. He said nothing, noting their boots, the caps, the scared and brooding expressions. He opened the lower door. Inside was a low-ceilinged room with settles against the walls. There were benches at the trestle tables for the regulars, and wooden stools at the bar. The windows had wooden shutters. Behind the bar a door led to the kitchen where the turf fire made more yellow smoke. The residents' eyes watered, they'd never smelled turf before.

'Home at last, Phonsie. These are the visitors. I dare say they'll take a glass,' Phelim said in a grim tone.

Phonsie said nothing but walked behind the bar, setting up glasses, pulling the beer lever. Sylvie leaned over to say that Warden didn't like his residents to drink. Mac (the one with the broad shoulders) shouldn't touch alcohol ever. Phonsie narrowed his eyes.

'Is Warden the one with the beard? Where are the children? Is the orphanage Timothy's or not?'

He looked at his brother. They'd assumed Timothy was a man of substance owning a reputable school. Had he hoodwinked them? It was a penance to see that wee cripple with her thumbs in her withered lips. And all of them dumb, seemingly. A drop to drink might get their tongues moving, but the boss woman said no. The nerve of her, no sooner over the doorstep than giving out orders as if he were a servant. To spite her he poured a drink for the one with the broad shoulders. He had a thirst all right, no matter what their rules.

Phelim straightened some books in the corner, his back to the rest of them. Loveliness sidled up to him.

'Not to touch, little lady. Grown-ups only,' he said pulling a book from her hand. His books were not for general reading. He hoped they wouldn't all go poking into what wasn't their business. What a persecution she must be to have around day and night.

Loveliness went back to Cap. Mac held out his glass for more. The rest sat on the settles, watching their knees again.

'Please, Phonsie. No,' Sylvie said. She'd have to explain the rules since Tim appeared to be sulking again. He'd gone as dumb as the rest, presumably because Phelim had called her lovely. He should have stopped Phonsie from pouring out drink for Mac, not her. She'd noticed how both brothers reacted to the residents. Poor things, they couldn't help looking odd. She asked how many locals Phonsie served every day, trying to be pleasant, show interest.

'The soldiers come of a night. This is a mixed house you understand? We cater for all creeds, all kinds. Phelim and I have no prejudice have we, Pheelie?'

Phelim didn't reply, his mind on his open book.

'Where are the soldiers?'

'The other side of the hill.' Phonsie looked to the skyline behind the half open shutters. The sight of the military descending at night was something both brothers relished. Trade boomed then. They were close-knit partners, with Phelim the brains, himself the braun. Next winter they hoped to expand, if plans worked as anticipated.

Phelim shut his book sharply. 'Now little ones, come with Uncle. I'll take you to your caravans.'

He rattled the keys, stepping across the mud. After a wash and a bit to eat they might buck their ideas up. They might even talk.

'I'll leave you to unpack now. All said your morning prayers?'

He couldn't resist asking. Hoaxsters. Heathen lot.

Tim felt heavy inside. All hope of getting Sylvie to himself died. There were two vans, he was stuck with the men. Instead of a wife and a honeymoon he had that sickly Hemm in the bunk by him. Not to mention the other four. Mr Silk wouldn't speak outside England seemingly. It wasn't food and friendship he hungered for now, it was his lovely wife. The sooner she directed her energy towards him in place of the brutes the better they'd all be. She'd never teach them anything no matter how lofty her motives, this holiday had made that much clear. He'd finish what he'd set out to do, settle the monetary matters with Phelim, get what was due to him and head back. No sense in lingering about. The brutes wouldn't care, there was nothing here for them, nothing for him and Sylvie. He'd not liked the way Phelim had spoken to Sylvie, as if he'd not been present. On top of that he'd been struck speechless with disappointment when he'd seen Phelim had no television aerial, his wet roof only had smoke over it. How would they pass the time? Rain, isolation on a mountain in the home of suspicious cousins was a gloomy prospect. The men's van had a stove in it, some cooking pots but no Sylvie to cook for them. He sat on his bunk with the rest trying not to feel lonely, afraid. He tried to forget his howling stomach, tried not to sigh out loud.

In the ladies' van Sylvie grabbed Cap.

'Did you see those books that Phelim had in the bar? They were about gambling, I looked. Racing books. I think they gamble here. And Phonsie drinks I'm sure. What is this place, what have we got into? I don't trust Phonsie, he gave Mac drinks after I asked him not to.'

Cap rocked Loveliness. Her smile was superior. Trust Sylvie to get the wind up, suspicious cat. Not that Cap liked it here, not yet, but she'd wait and see. Not much fun about so far. She stowed Loveliness's other gym tunic under one of the bunks. Loveliness looked at herself in her doll's mirror, applying her rose madder rouge.

That night in the bar the visitors felt outcast. They sipped glasses of club orange. Phonsie topped Mac's glass from a bottle of something colourless. All of them would have preferred to stay in the vans, away from the stares, winks and nudges of the hillside people. Phonsie seemed to expect them to stay there, he'd taken a fancy to Mac. They pulled their caps down over their brows, lowering their heads again, tucking their boots under the settles which they drew up close, huddling for solidarity. For the first time in her life Cap felt ashamed of Loveliness, though she said nothing. Tim looked at Sylvie pleadingly. If she'd just smile at him. He pined for television and food, he pined for her affection most. Was he too late? Sylvie was feeling a mixture of rage and doubt. She pitied the residents trying their best to conform. She overheard a hillsider saying they should all be behind bars. Why didn't Tim answer back, defend the residents instead of staring at her with a moony expression? Why didn't he show more pluck? The hillsiders had narrow bony faces, whispering behind their hands. There were no womenfolk with them.

Phonsie was behind the bar, busily pulling pints. She asked him where Phelim was.

'I'm not his keeper, Marm. Nor is he mine, for all we're close-knit. He's rarely in of an evening, the bar is my domain. He manages the books, sees to lettings, orders the grub. I could do with some help here.' He looked meaningfully at Mac. Their busiest time would be soon, when the soldiers from over the hill arrived.

'I think our residents should go to bed. Mac can't do bar work. I told you he shouldn't drink. He shouldn't go near drink. We've had a long day, Phonsie. Where has Phelim gone?'

'Time enough. Wait now till you see the soldiers, after the hillsiders leave. The bar comes alive when they arrive, you'll see for yourself, Marm.'

'What is that short drink you serve? We're not on show you know. Those people keep staring over at us. What's the drink?'

'Power?'

'Not whisky, that other, the one you gave to Mac.'

'A wee something I make for myself. For my friends. It's

quiet here, off season, the folk only want to be friendly, Marm.'

'Poteen? That's illegal. I've heard of it. It sends people mad. You mean you have a still? Mac mustn't . . .'

'Whisht now, here come the military.'

'You mustn't give Mac drink. We stick to Warden's rules.'

'Don't be talking about that. The soldiers, look.'

The uniformed men stamped in, shaking the rain from their capes, stamping their boots free of mud. The way over the hill was stony. They had shouting voices, calling Phonsie, wanting his mountain dew. They ribbed him about his sweater, about his yellow hair, his accent. Singing started. The bar rang out with noise. Mac smiled at last, dribbling over his chinpiece. He'd like to help Phonsie, his legs wouldn't hold him up. Warden slept. Tim was upset. Mac was letting the party down. If Warden awoke he'd see Mac, the sight might be too much for him. Tim leaned over the bar to speak to Phonsie, trying not to breathe the liquor smell. Phonsie must understand, by serving Mac he was breaking Harmony regulations. He wished Phelim were present, he trusted Phonsie less than his brother.

'How long since *you* left Ireland, Timothy? A poor countryman you are. I'd like to know how the likes of you found Phelim.'

'He found me, Cousin, surely you knew? He wrote first about our Uncle's testimony.' Was Phonsie ignorant of Uncle's will, ignorant of his death too? Did he not know why they'd come. Phonsie was wrong to serve that evil stuff. This spot was so remote, Tim didn't like the soldiers either. He'd had no idea they were so near to a military zone. He'd overheard talk of arson, attacks by rubber bullets, looting. Which side did his Cousins favour? Where was their loyalty? More importantly, how did they dare to serve such appalling food? That dinner earlier had been atrocious. (Iron banners he believed those potatoes were called.) The meals would kill them if not the low company and wet. He felt friendless without Hemm awake to back him up. He missed Silk's smiling support. This was the time to speak, to show Sylvie that he had leadership and drive, to speak up clearly and well. He must confer with her first. He'd forget jealousy, base instincts, forget television, ignore everything but flight. They were at risk, particularly Mac. No knowing what Phonsie might do, he might start giving Silk liquor or Warden himself. If only he had Hemm's car he'd simply drive them away.

'I leave the business side to Phelim. A great man for the moneybags is Pheelie. He only told me you were coming this morning. He'll let you know what you owe in due course.'

A fear crept round Tim's heart. *He* owe Phelim? What did Phonsie mean?

'Please, Sylvie, I must speak with you. Don't say No, I must. Can you come to the men's van now?'

'No need. I'm as worried as you are. We can't stay here. It's ... they are devious. I heard what Phonsie said. I distrust everyone and everything here.'

'We'll leave. I'll tell Phelim tomorrow. It's worse than the back of nowhere. I'm so relieved you feel as I do. We're in agreement then?'

They smiled into each other's faces, united by common unease. Horrific food, political danger, corrupt brothers serving illegal drink, brothers not even trusting each other, it was all dreadful. They were so far from home. Sylvie put her hand in Tim's. They would have kissed but for the red faces of the soldiery and the pale residents. They would leave at dawn next day after a sleep in the glossy vans which would give some sort of shelter from the beating rain. Never had the roof of St Harmony seemed so safe, so desirable.

Next morning Sylvie knocked at the gents' van with a fearful face. She'd woken alone, Cap and Loveliness were missing. Their bunks in the ladies' van were bare.

❧ Ten

Sylvie put the blame on Phonsie. Tim blamed Phelim. Between them the cousins ran a questionable business, kept illegal hours, serving raw spirits to their own hillsiders as well as the military men. The legacy was in question. Their food was the final straw. Could it have been hunger that lured Cap and Loveliness from the van at dawn? Sylvie's mouth trembled. She'd slept heavily, she hadn't heard them leave. If anything happened to Cap she'd never get over it. If Cap was dead she'd have died without learning to sew. The other residents looked worse not better after their sleep. Where were their lady members? Where was their Uncle host? Phonsie alone was smirking. It would take more than this gang of renegades to upset him. He cut up crusts of bread. His turf fire had gone out. Let them eat old bread, cold tea. They'd run out of milk as well.

'I'm frantic about them. Don't you care, Phonsie, that they're missing?'

'I know my brother, Marm. We understand one another. And don't be fretting, the two . . . girls will be back.' Them and their nasty scents.

'But they don't know the district. I blame you, Phonsie. We're strangers.'

'Blame me? Why? Me that welcomed you? It'll be a while before I welcome your kind again, that's if there are more like you which I doubt. Hooligans. The clothes of you.

Blame *me*? Don't think I didn't see those two flirting, giving the army the eye. They shouldn't be let loose. I saw you too, Sylvie, flirting, oh yes.'

'The eye? Eye where?'

'In the bar. Last night.'

'That's a lie, Phonsie. I'd have noticed anything wrong.'

'No one calls me a liar without regretting it, Timothy. I seed them with my two eyes. Ask Phelim. And I'm not worrying about Phelim, he can look after himself, he often takes a night away.'

'Night away where? I have to speak to Phelim. It's urgent.' Tim dropped his voice. Both brothers needed handling quietly. He regretted calling Phonsie a liar. But Sylvie wasn't a flirt. Such an idea, with those red-faced soldiers too.

'Sure dog racing surely. At the track at the foot of the hill.'

'But you don't encourage him do you? Gambling is taboo at Harmony. Gambling is irresponsible.'

'Taboo is it? Irresponsible? Is that a fact? And didn't I see with my two eyes a game of cards going. The men were playing at the cards, playing for money they were, I seed them yesterday.'

'Ah ... that was Happy Families, a kiddies' game, Phonsie. Just a bit of fun. Relaxation.'

'Aye, and well suited to your kind. Kiddies. You played for cash, don't try to say different. Not that I care either way.'

The money hadn't been real, Tim was too shamed to tell. No one had enjoyed the game, they hadn't spoken or smiled as they'd pointed to their cards. No one had won or lost, they hadn't finished the round. Silk had produced the money from his cotton pocket. Tim saw Every slip a coin between his gums, he'd not sucked one himself. The money was probably chocolate, Silk believed in sweets as a seal of friendship. He couldn't tell Phonsie that, it seemed silly.

97

'Loveliness. Where is my Loveliness?' Warden suddenly wailed; the first words he had uttered since entering this grey wet land. He'd endured a sea crossing sitting on a bench, had been pushed up a mountain, made to stretch his bones on a bunk in some white tin shed. He'd witnessed infantry men carousing, had heard them shout and sing in uniform that would pass no parade inspection. He'd drunk stewed black tea. These things were nothing compared to his present pain. His light, his pride, his heart of a rose was absent without leave.

'She's upped and gone, old codger. Run off with the one you call Cap.' And a good riddance to the both of them in Phonsie's view. He looked at Warden's hands. He'd be the next to leave and his ticket would be one way. He swilled the teapot under the tap. Why waste fresh leaves on hooligans? He'd brew up when Phelim got back, a strong pot for the both of them.

'Search partee,' Mr Silk whispered, breaking his Irish silence. Sole cracked his fingers, wishing he felt brave. He deplored the state of the bar furniture, he longed to get hold of some string. Mac licked his lip. Every scratched deep inside his clothes. No one had removed any clothing for their night in the glossy van. They were ready to search right away.

'You don't know the hillside. There's a wind got up,' Phonsie warned. Impertinent dirty lot.

'Wait everyone. No sense in rushing up the mountain without a plan first,' Tim said. The residents must assemble now by the vans. They must listen to his instructions. Firstly, keep calm. It was possible that the two ladies had gone for an early stroll. Though not probable, Sylvie interrupted. Loveliness was a poor walker, Cap hated any exercise, besides look at the weather, darker, windier, wetter. Tim still thought there was a chance, he might have walked himself had there been a caff handy. The thought of chocolate money awoke his sweet tooth, especially after that bitter tea. Now then, take courage, start off searching in twos. Understood? They must climb the hill behind the bar, at all costs staying in pairs, they mustn't separate, they mustn't go down the far side. That was the soldiers' territory. They must search in the wet heather, look under hanging rocks. Cap and Loveliness might be hurt. They must keep shouting 'Hal-loo.' Like this. His voice sounded weak, born off by the wind blowing over the hill. No matter, practise, have a try. The residents called, pitching their voices variously, opening their mouths to the wind. The hens turned their beaks to them, the unseen dog howled. They began to feel braver. It was the first sound Every, Sole and Mac had uttered on holiday. 'Hal-loo. Hal-loo.'

'Hal-loo. Can I join in? How about the one with the broad shoulders giving a hand in the bar?' Phonsie called from the half door. A cigarette hung from his mocking mouth, his hair was flat with rain.

'Thank you, Phonsie. I'm sorry. No.'

'Hal-loo. Tell me for why?'

'My residents live by rules. You wouldn't understand, you're an outsider. No alcohol, no twosomes.'

'What's up with you, Timothy? You're only after putting them into twos. I'm telling you the hill is dangerous, especially near the top. Let the one with the broad shoulders . . .'

'No.'

'Oh let him, Tim. Let Mac stay here with Phonsie.' The runaways might come back while they were gone. Sylvie noted Warden. Oh dear.

Warden was sobbing openly. It was unmanly; he couldn't stop. The rest looked uncomfortable. They patted him, they straightened his cap. Mr Silk gave his cane top a rub. Tim pushed ahead. They must hurry, they must keep calling. Hemm would perk up when they started. They'd leave Mac, risk him getting intoxicated. Now, hold hands with your partners, remember the rallying call. Their Wellingtons slipped in the mud. The dog howled again. They were glad they'd been warned off drinking, look what it did to Mac. They'd be leaving the hillside for good soon, they'd call Hal-loo with a will. The horrid Uncles would soon be a memory, likewise the food and wet.

Footsteps were coming towards them. The Uncle in green, with the specs, came tramping through the gate. His feet were slow, one shoe had no lace, his pocket-lining hung torn against one leg. He hadn't shaved. He spoke.

'What's up with you now? Where do you think you're going?'

'Cousin P, where were you? Loveliness and Cap are lost. Your glasses are cracked, what happened?'

'Lost? Gone, are they? My, my, that is sad.'

'We're very worried. We must find them before we leave.'

'Leave? You can't. We have a lot to talk over, we must discuss business, you can't go away like that.'

'*You* left us, Cousin. Why did you leave when we needed you?'

'I do as I please. It's my home and my country. I went dog racing, any objection?' It was time to stand up to the Englishers with their royal highness airs, their do's, their don'ts, their reproaches, imagining they were always right. Yes, he did bet on dogs, his brother liked a drink. They weren't changing, no intentions. Timothy appeared to think the world must keep in step to suit him. He was no saint, far from it, his school wasn't his at all. Swindling hoaxster with his heathen lot. What gave Timothy the right to change anyone, or manage others when he couldn't manage himself? The whole gang should be run off the premises, not just yet though, in his and Phonsie's good time.

'Cousin, look, your pocket. It's empty, you've lost money. Gambling is irresponsible.'

Tim felt Sylvie touching him, warning him to watch his

tongue. No sense in antagonising Phelim, they were wasting the time they should spend searching. Better not criticize now. Besides, they'd come on a free holiday, expecting money, they weren't so noble themselves.

Phelim mopped his brow. His jaunty hat feather was gone. He'd been robbed on all sides. He wouldn't argue, he'd get back to the comfort of his racing books, to the bar's peace, the fire, to Phonsie and fresh-brewed tea.

Warden moved his lips. 'Loveliness. Loveliness.' He'd forgotten the rallying call. Sole grasped him by the elbows to keep him from keeling over. The walk up to the soldiers' path behind the bar was rough. They were glad to hold hands in twos.

'Hurry. Hurry residents,' Tim urged, waving his hands, urging them faster.

The sky got darker as they neared the top, the walking stonier, muddier. They left the track in search of less sharpness and wet to the soles of their Wellingtons. Like soaked migrants they longed to rest. They didn't feel brave at all. Tim called a halt. They leaned against some boulders, straining their eyes up and round.

'Tim, have you noticed that none of them speak? Since we left England no one says a word.'

'Hemm has. Silk said something. I have noticed though, and I worry. Oh Sylvie, where can they be? I feel so guilty, we shouldn't have come. I know how much you liked Cap.'

'Don't feel guilty. You've been good, Tim. You didn't want to bring them, you did it for me. It's the older men I worry about most. We'd better go on hadn't we? I expect we will find them.'

At the top the couples sat down, not caring about mud and stones. They panted, their tiredness and fear was replaced by faint triumph. It had been a tidy climb, Every and Warden had managed particularly well. They raised their chins to the grey sky, resting.

Warden heard it first, the sound born on the wind, he

cupped his ear with his hand, he scrambled up, brushing Sole's hand aside. Then they all heard it, like music, a human call. They waited, the sound got louder. There was a lorry or a heavy engine the far side of the hill. Tim told Warden to sit again while he reconnoitred. He craned over a boulder. Scrubby bushes blocked his view down the far side of the hill. He heard shouts, a burst of song, the noise of the engine again. A Land Rover climbed into view. It stopped below in a clearing. Tim could see clearly then as a soldier got out, lifting something resembling a bundle of clothes, setting it down in the clearing. The bundle moved. Another soldier lifted a smaller bundle. There was loud singing. 'Oh little town of Bethlehem, Without a city wall.' Sylvie moved to Tim's side. The others followed.

'Oh Tim. It's Cap. And Loveliness. They're drunk.'

'Merciful God, what is to become of us?' For the first time in twenty-five years Tim crossed himself. They watched the soldiers move back to the Land Rover, having dumped the two ladies in the mud. They turned, making a rude sign at them before they drove away. Cap lifted her head, seeing their faces at the top.

'You all dead up there? Snap out of it, Warden, old cock.'

Warden could watch no more, he slid to the ground again, his beard resting on his cane. He slept. Sole, with grave kindness settled him more comfortably, moving loose stones and a rock, making room for his gammy leg. He understood Warden, understood his shame. Warden would rather lose Loveliness for ever than have her return like this. With sleep and time he'd forget.

'Search partee happy,' Mr Silk said softly.

Every scratched again.

Cap shouted, swaying her shaggy head. She accused them of being a pack of bloody police dogs. She didn't want no lecture either. She wanted to get back to St Harm's. Sylvie put her arm round her, pressing her cheek to Cap's. Loveliness's grey curls were straight. With her tunic pinned to the ankle buttons of her gaiters she looked like a glove puppet. Both had lost their woolly caps. The noise of the Land Rover became fainter until they couldn't hear it.

There was the problem of getting the two down the hill, as well as Warden. Tim picked up Loveliness who wriggled and squirmed, pushing her mouth at his face. He felt her wiry bones, smelled her breath and her snaggle teeth. He felt weary, sick of the lot of them. Mr Silk and Sylvie persuaded Cap to walk between them with her arms about their waists. She was the noisiest. Sole gently shook Warden. Come now, time to descend. He half pushed and half carried him. When they neared flatter ground by the Hillside bar he lifted him over his back.

'We mustn't let Phelim see. Let's leave now, we needn't say goodbye. He mustn't see Cap like this.'

'We mustn't go without Mac. Let's hope he's not drunk as well. Besides, there's the will. I must get that settled with Phelim.' After all they'd been through Tim wasn't leaving without a detailed promise in writing. He didn't trust Phelim to send the money on, he must have that assurance. He'd have earned every penny after this escapade. He told Sylvie to take Cap and Loveliness to the ladies' van, to get them to swallow aspirin, get them to sleep a while. Then to join him in the bar to witness what Phelim said.

Sylvie went to the van for the last time. Soon this would be a bad memory. She pushed them both on to their bunks. Warden tapped at the door with a dry-fingered hand. There were tears in his voice.

'Please, is she quite quite well? You're sure, Sylvie, she's all right? Let me help pack her gubbins, my little girl's things.'

'She's still drunk. You shouldn't come into this van. Oh all right, but don't waken either of them.'

She picked her way across the Hillside yard. They'd go now. She never wanted to mention Tim's Cousins again, or the name of Hillside. They'd come for a holiday, they'd had no fun at all. She heard Tim shouting in the bar, then she heard Phonsie. They'd get Mac and go.

'Who are you calling "no one"? It's you and your hooligans that are no one. You weren't too proud to sponge. Living like lords over here, out to grab, we're well rid of you. Not lifting a hand, none of yous. Grabbing my booze when you could.'

'Meaning me I suppose?' Mac joined in with a snarl. 'I'm glad to be leaving. I'm not happy, for all your home-made hooch.'

'Aye but you drank it didn't you? And nothing in return. Louser.' His poteen was famed. Offering it to Mac was worse than pouring it down the drain.

'Who are you calling "louser"?' Mac whipped a knife out, menacing Phonsie round the face, just missing his slab of fringe.

'Now, Mac, not here please.' Tim pulled his arm.

'Mac, put that away,' Sylvie said quietly. He wasn't drunk, mercifully. His knife fell making no sound. She picked it up, put it in her holdall. Long ago she'd wondered if his knives were dangerous. It was a rubber knife. She felt protective, she'd take on the world for her residents. She'd got to know their weaknesses, knew that they wore a mask for the world to cover their confusions. Mac liked to appear ferocious, inside he was tender, afraid. They mustn't know, no one had seen the knife bend in her hand. Tim was shouting at Phelim.

'I'm not wasting my time squabbling. I want to know about the will.'

'Look you, Timothy. You come over with a gang of terrorists, expecting to live scot free. You mess up our caravans with card games, your boots make work for Phonsie. I want something for expenses before we discuss any wills. You have the audacity to ask me for money. It's me that is asking you.'

'But Phelim, Uncle's will. The inheritance, your

letters . . .'

'Letters? What about them? It's cash I need from you. I met you at the boat. I bought your train tickets. You ate the best, you've had every class of comfort.'

'Comfort? You call that van comfortable? That food fit for a dog? Phelim, is there a legacy? It appears that all you have on your mind is dog racing. You squandering no one, yes, no one. How much is coming to me? I want to know now.'

'Tim, please say goodbye now.'

'Wait, Sylvie, I must get this settled.'

'Settled? I'll settle you, Timothy.' Phelim raised his fist.

From the ladies' van came a terrible cry. Phelim lowered his arm. If one of them was hurting his hound they'd be sorry.

'Tim, it's Warden. He's screaming. Quickly.'

In the ladies' van Cap still snored oblivious to the noise. Warden was sitting on the edge of Loveliness's bunk, her small figure stretched before him. The gym tunic was unpinned from the gaiters, the hem pulled back to the waist. The child's double-knit bloomers were down. The scrap-book pictures had lied, Loveliness Marker was no Miss. Between the tiny thighs spotted with red was a dolly-sized penis.

'Oh Loveliness. Oh Love. Where are you now my love?'

Loveliness saw them watching and wept.

✾ Eleven

With the exception of one the residents had found their voices. Their tongues were unstuck because they were going home. Their dark experiences were over, they'd think twice about holidays again. Tim had been tricked and deceived. There'd never been any inheritance, no dead Uncle, nothing. They'd not been welcomed for themselves but for what Phelim and Phonsie hoped to get. The brothers imagined Tim was rich, owner of an orphanage. They'd no use for St Harmony now. The residents supposed the brothers made a practice of sending letters to strangers, hoping to get rich. They would leave now gladly. They could smile and talk again.

At the last Phelim called Tim back to the bar. 'Could you ever let me have a fiver? Please, Timothy.'

They crossed the yard with sunny faces. Phelim and Phonsie refused to shake hands, watching them leave from the half door, not speaking. Warden was last as usual. At the gate he felt something bite him. The dog guarding the illicit still rushed from the outhouse, biting him through his trousers. The brothers didn't move, refusing to call the dog off, refusing to help Warden who called them. He tried to jump, tried to step up his knees to release the snapping jaws. Sole and Every helped, beating the dog's ears with the silvery topped cane. The rest pulled Warden to safety. Loveliness hadn't stopped crying, her face stiff as a marionette. The noise of Warden and Loveliness had sobered Cap. She had adjusted Loveliness's clothing but couldn't stem her tears. Sylvie had wanted to ask the brothers for aspirin, for water and bandages. Tim refused. They'd carry on, the brothers were cantankerous, they'd give Warden first aid at the station. When they lowered the brown tweed trousers they found the skin nicked by the dog's teeth and a brindled hair or two. Warden still moaned. The train was late. They'd got soaked through again.

Sole said he thought Phelim had a sad look round the eyes, as if he'd miss them. Both brothers were wifeless, childless, it could be that they envied Tim and Sylvie secretly. The human heart was complex, they might be kind inside. Cap scoffed at Sole, she knew men didn't she? She was concerned about Warden.

'He's got spots, red ones, did you see? I got some and all. And Loveliness.'

'I have been bitten too,' Sole turned back his cuffs to show a rash round his wrists.

Each resident exhibited spots dotted about his limbs.

'Fleas,' Every explained. They bit in clusters, he had experience of bites, his friend who lived in Limerick had suffered the same way.

'They don't only bite in Limerick. You get fleas everywhere. We've had no fun here. Loveliness has been exposed, there ain't no cash, Warden got bit, we all of us got fleas. You meant well, Tim, the Hillside might be a nice place in summer. Sorry we went off with the soldiers. I wanted a bit of life.'

'Did you know about Loveliness all along, Cap?' Sylvie wished that she had been kinder to her. Poor little thing, she had suffered appalling loss of face after a life based on a lie. She wondered if they should continue to call her 'she'. The bites on her bendy legs were the worst Sylvie had ever seen.

'I never cared. Love wanted to be a woman, Gawd knows why but she did. Far as I'm concerned she's a person. She's

human, not a freak. She wanted to change her life. I don't
care, she's my friend. Look at her, poor Babe. I blame
Warden, dirty old sod.'

'She talked about woman's liberation, didn't you hear
her, Tim?'

'I never paid much attention.' Tim felt uncomfortable,
wishing he had never stared at Loveliness. Hemm had more
than paid the price of passion, ending up dog-bitten,
spotted and scorned. He'd no interest in male or female liberation himself, so long as he got Sylvie back and his party
back to St Harmony. The holiday had been packed with un-
fortunate discovery. Cap explained that Loveliness didn't
really enjoy being stared and peered at, particularly when
the peerers were embarrassed. Dressing up, having tantrums gave her courage. She'd been happy in the circus.
Cap understood her.

'If you thought so much of her why take her over the
hill?' Sylvie was resentful. Because of Loveliness Cap had
little time for her. They'd not been alone since the time Cap
spilled polish on to her.

'I pinned her tunic down, I tried to give eye to her. Them
soldiers laughed. She wanted a bit of life, same as me. I done
what I could.' No one had seen Cap cry. Her smile was like
a grimace.

'Leave her. Don't pester. My fault,' Warden whispered
with eyes closed. He was to blame, not Cap, he should have
been more vigilant. And now he felt so tired. The indignity
of his bottom being bared was part of the price, his punish-
ment. The military in this war-torn land brought no credit.
He'd seen decency flouted. He'd not found the proud race
he'd expected, their retreat wasn't proud either, they'd
nothing to be proud about. He scratched with a flaking
finger.

The residents looked better. They'd turned their caps
about rakishly, moving with purpose. Yesterday's sleeping
ghosts were gone. At the boat they raided the gangplank

with prancing step. Sole and Every helped Warden. Tim covered him with his coat. He'd wanted to book cabins for everyone. Dear people, they were worth being made poor for. Nor could he really blame Hemm, he'd only done what many people secretly wanted to do. Curiosity was a common failing. He'd buy chips and sausages when they docked. Hemm must have medical attention. The residents refused the cabins, preferring to stick together. Talking was such a great pleasure, they couldn't do it enough. Every spoke of work, he would carve anything. He didn't regret his sandwich boards, 'Umbrellas old, umbrellas new' had served him. He had his family now, he was ready to turn to wood. Sole spoke of the dog at Hillside which should have been kept leashed, either that or hung by a noose. Mac said why not knife it? They sat round Warden, careful not to bang his leg or touch his bitten part. They chafed his sore fingers gently. Mr Silk beamed. Sitting in lotus style while breathing and thinking of peace was twice as good in company. Loveliness turned her grey head from one to the other, not speaking yet. Mac was afraid the dog getting loose had been his fault. He'd not bolted the door when Phelim sent him for more illicit drink. He'd like to try wine-making one day. The rest nodded, they understood. Drink should be open, shared. They looked at Tim, what did he think? And what were his future plans? It wasn't his fault that they were going home early, what would he do next? Was he still set on working in television? They didn't care about viewing, why didn't he stay with them? Tim went silent with joy. They needed him, he'd not been wasting his time. Pies, eggy and plain, with Sylvie working in a frilly apron was a bright dream to give up. He still believed his destiny lay in commerce. He was worried about Hemm. He said he'd wait until Hemm was well before taking definite steps. Warden didn't speak, but he heard. He gave Tim a look of great sweetness and strength. He looked years younger in the face. The night passed.

Snow was falling when they reached their own country. They hadn't slept, they weren't tired at all, nor did they feel hungry. They raised their faces as if the sun was shining, feeling the snow touch their teeth. Every forgot to cover his gums, they smiled into the sky. St Harmony drew them like gold, each one longed for his or her mattress and privacy. They'd see the gold tree again, get their feet under the kitchen table, relax and be themselves.

They reached the door. Loveliness gulped, rushing under the stairs.

'Don't go after her,' Cap warned. 'I know her best. She wants her scrapbooks, pretend we never left. She'll never feel the same. People know.'

Tim said he'd light a fire. Sole and he pulled the boards that covered the grate away. The notice on Warden's bulletin board had fallen. There wasn't too much soot. He asked for wood chopping volunteers.

Every and Sole made a good pile from the wood in the attic where Warden had made his bed. Since he'd moved up he'd never been the same. His old room had been more central, the attic was broken and cold. He oughtn't to go there again. Cap helped Sylvie in the kitchen. Loveliness stayed under the stairs. They laid Warden on a mattress before the blazing fire. They felt virtuous and fine, caring for their leader who had cared for them. They'd pamper him now until the doctor came. It didn't seem likely that he'd ever drive again. He was so trembly. They arranged his pillow to face the golden tree.

'I'm starting a hammock for him, it will be ready for his convalescence.' Sole fetched his netting needle, his mesh stick and twine. His knuckly fingers flew. The residents asked how he'd climb into it; he couldn't manage the stairs, much less a hammock.

'Don't worry,' Sole said.

Sylvie said they shouldn't wake Warden, he could eat later, that they'd sit round him for their meal. Under the

110

cover of tapping forks and biting teeth Tim asked her if he could stay, did she want him there? He couldn't leave Hemm now, after all they'd gone through. It would be a while before he would be well enough to command. Should he remain?

'I was hoping you would. I'd hate it on my own. Especially tonight. There's so much to think about. My bed is big enough. Stay.'

Tim reddened. He wouldn't think of it now. His wife, his Sylvie, touching her, exploring. Her lovely body, his. Beginning again, but better, a real beginning. He wanted her for herself, not because she was like that nun. He forced his voice to be practical. Wait until they were alone, in the official bed.

'That's settled then. I think Hemm will be a lot better tomorrow. Now, Sylvie, about the social security people. Ought not the sex of Loveliness to be recorded officially?'

She said that her pension was made out to Miss. They should respect her privacy. Sylvie agreed with Cap, people mattered more than the labels the world gave them. Whether men, women or children, feelings and heart came first.

'Harmonee happy,' said Mr Silk, putting his plate away.

The flames were lovely and warm, nobody wanted to move. They'd stay and watch over Warden, sleeping his deep sweet sleep. Tim would ring for the doctor first thing in the morning. Warden had never approved of doctors' medicine, they'd watch, hold vigil. Tim's thoughts kept straying to that bed, Hemm's ill fortune had brought good for him. The residents didn't blame Warden, it was bad luck that he'd been caught peeking. Curiosity of that kind wasn't their concern. Whatever Loveliness was like under her clothes didn't matter. She was still Loveliness, and a nuisance a lot of the time. Bad luck had helped bring each of them to St Harmony. Once there each one thought of himself. The sex of Loveliness was less important than food, warmth, consideration.

'Poor old sod, I feel sorry for him,' Cap said, tucking the sheet under his beard.

They switched the light off, huddling in a bunch, whispering so that he shouldn't wake. Snow fell down the chimney, hissing over the flames.

'Is that a dog outside? Did you hear, something whined?'

The flames made strange shadows on the door behind them. They didn't see Warden die.

They raised their voices when they realized. Too late, he'd gone, he'd left them. They howled from sadness, they howled from regret at their ingratitude, from sorrow from scorning him, from shame at flouting his rules. They howled because they'd not loved him until it was too late. They'd never make amends. Stiff, wall-eyed as a dead animal, he was beyond hearing, his acid breath was still. They'd never hear that cane tapping, that voice cautioning them to avoid drink, cards, laziness or disappearing in twos. They wiped their noses with their holiday hankies and slept.

Tim went to the telephone where Every slept. There were arrangements to make, the doctor to ring, funerals to think about. Who were his relatives and friends? The neighbourhood had always given St Harmony a wide berth. Who would mourn the funny old boy except his own residents?

'It's no good, Tim. The telephone is broken again.'

'Again? It's always broken. Poor Hemm, he had a lot to contend with.'

'We'll look in his briefcase. He must have had relatives, he went to the West County a lot.'

It felt wrong to pry in his business. His tracts and files were for his eyes alone. He saw nothing now, they could look and he wouldn't know. Just the same they went to the kitchen for privacy, away from the presence of death. The residents woke, they followed Tim and Sylvie, they wanted to watch Tim pull out the secret files.

112

'Look at Loveliness's first.' Sylvie thought Warden might have known more about Loveliness than he pretended. Her file might give more clues about his unsual nature. He'd been more of dark horse than they knew. Tim stood with the file open in his hand. Sylvie took it. The columns that she'd ruled were empty. Warden had written nothing. Name, sex, married or single, date of birth (if known), next of kin (if agreeable), previous residence (if remembered), jobs held, general progress and behaviour were left blank, unrecorded. The other files were the same. For years Warden had pretended to write in them or sat staring at empty pages.

'Look in the tracts, go on. Look in *Striving to Grow*.'

Tim and Sylvie were glad that the residents were poor readers or didn't read at all. They were afraid of what they'd find.

'It's not a tract at all. A lot of telephone numbers. No names, just numbers. Did he make calls often?'

The residents agreed that he had. They'd all heard him dialling at night when he slept downstairs off the hall, though the telephone was often broken.

'Open the other tracts, *In Search of Unity*, *Flog and Slog*. He must have had friends somewhere.'

'Sylvie. This must be burned.'

Inside *In Search of Unity* were records of telephone conversations in Warden's crabbed hand. Sylvie looked. She put her hand to her mouth. Cap leaned over, reading aloud slowly. She read what Warden had said to a Mrs Cummin. What he had threatened a Miss Seymour with. The fear he had instilled in Miss Vent.

'He was a dirtier old sod than I thought. He was loopy. Poor Loveliness.'

From under the stairs came a screech again. Loveliness appeared.

'That's Warden's business. Leave them. Put the books away.'

'Warden is dead, Loveliness.'

'I know. I heard. I knew he would die.'

'Did you know he made disgusting telephone calls to ladies?'

'I wanted him to stop. I tidied his desk, I used to break the telephone wire with a knife. Warden. Oh Warden.'

'I suspected you of vandalism, Loveliness. And you were trying to help. I misjudged you.' Sylvie spoke with difficulty. Loveliness had born a great burden, protecting Warden as well as keeping her own secret. He had lost grace, fallen from their esteem. On top of the holiday it was hard to bear. Her boss was a voyeur, a maker of obscene calls. She asked if Loveliness knew where he went in the West Country.

'Look in the tract called *Flog*.'

They were afraid of fresh felony. Sole opened it. He stared. A slow reader, they thought he'd forgotten his alphabet. He spoke at last. It seemed that Warden had another charity in the country. This second interest was a rest centre for dogs, an institution where hounds could live out their days. Animals suffering from illness, heart conditions or plain old age could stay until they died. A feature of the retreat were green lawns, spacious grounds.

'Did you know about this as well, Loveliness?'

'I may be small but I listen. Warden trusted me. Alone I called him Daddie. He liked that. He never took advantage until . . . until.' Her lips trembled, she put in her thumbs. She went on to say that she'd known about the Twilight Rest Centre. She was going to see it in the summer.

'This makes a difference. He wasn't all bad. Perhaps those calls weren't as obscene as we think.'

'Obscene? What's that?' Loveliness frowned. They shouldn't speak against Daddie.

'It means rude. Upsetting. He was good about old dogs. I can see why he hated gambling. Racing made the dogs ill. He was good and bad, like most people. A mixture.'

114

'Love ruled his actions, Sylvie. I knew Daddie. He loved dogs more than most folk.' Once Loveliness started words poured from her lips. She took out her thumbs. She looked more like the pictures in her books because she had listeners. She'd miss Daddie more than anyone. He used to like her talking, there was trust between them. He'd hated animals except for hounds. For her sake he'd let the cats stay, did they know that? His money went to the upkeep of the hounds. He'd loved her pictures, she was his golden charm. He'd made her cubby hole, gentleman that he was. Why did they say 'obscene'?

When she stopped they were quiet. Life was upended for all of them. With no one to flout or laugh at what would they do all day?

The fire fell in the grate. Someone should stay with the corpse.

'And we'll hide the tracts and records. They're of no interest to anyone.'

'Burn them. Burn everything.'

The fire roared. The blank records, *Striving to Grow*, *In Search of Unity* went up page by page, lighting the hall again, where Warden lay stiff and straight. Tim kept *Flog* in the briefcase, a proof of Hemm's altruism, proof that he had a sound heart. They'd get in touch with the Twilight. The staff would want to know of his demise.

They sat by him until light, watching his beard and silvery topped cane wink in the flames. He'd no need of his car now, or the hammock or golden tree.

☙ Twelve

Tim insisted on going to the Twilight retreat in the West Country before they did anything else. They mustn't proceed with the day's arrangements until they had been there first. The person in charge of it might know if Hemm had relatives, or he might have friends near the Twilight. If Loveliness was right, if he had preferred hounds to people his will would probably favour the Twilight. If he had died intestate then Harmony would have a claim. Secretly he wanted to delay Hemm's last exit. Once the doctor signed that death warrant, officialdom would rule. He and Sylvie would be left with the residents. They couldn't look after themselves, they would pine and fade on their own. Sylvie said they should wait, deaths should be registered quickly, it was the law. Tim got his way. The residents would be all the better for a trip in the red Ford. A spin would settle their nerves. They'd be back soon after noon. An hour or so made no difference, nothing could bring Warden Hemm back. A look at the Twilight would jolly them. He'd been full of surprises at the end, before he left for good. The care of dogs seemed a curious hobby. Tim was curious himself about the place.

On Sole's advice they let the fire die down. A corpse was better in a cold temperature. He showed them how to wash Warden. Each of the men took a limb or a part, lathering and rinsing, having dabbed at the dark bites with Cap's piece of rosy soap. Loveliness offered her scent. She and Cap tidied the hall, cleaning the tennis table for Warden. The men placed him on it with the golden tree at his feet. Loveliness pinned the miraculous medal that she'd stolen from Phelim on Daddie's pyjamas. He looked sweet when they'd finished, wearing the benign expression he had worn for Tim on the boat, and smelling lovely.

Sole stayed with him. Sole knew a lot about death. A corpse should be washed properly, someone should sit there then. He sat on his orange box, his netting needle, mesh stick and twine by his hands.

'I've had experience of death too during my perambulations. My friend in Limerick . . .'

'We don't want to hear no more about Limerick, Every. Sole got on well with Warden, he's the one to stay.' Cap settled Warden's hair with her broken-toothed comb.

The ride in the red Ford was bracing. The cold refreshed them, though they tried to keep mournful for appearance's sake. A drive was soothing, you didn't have to think. The wheels crunched on the snow, blackening it in streaks. Marking a white world gave you a feeling of power. They'd enjoy everything they could see in the West Country, start being miserable on the journey home. The sun was out. Mr Silk clasped his lemon-toned fingers over his stomach, inhaling deeply. Sir Hemm had joined his ancestors, an occasion to celebrate once the tears had dried. For Tim the countryside was better than a candlelit cake, brittle, waiting, new. He thrilled at the feeling of Sylvie's knee, warm, touching his. He moved, she didn't pull away. He'd not felt like this since his honeymoon. And this time he was confident. When the time came to lie in the official bed he knew she'd not pull away. She'd not have dislike, fear in her face, she never would again. His heart beat with hope, anticipation, joy. Syl-vee. Syl-vee.

The residents started singing. Sylvie turned. They could hum, loud singing wasn't fitting after the happening late last night. They looked crestfallen, but forgot her reproof, words broke from their mouths in spite of themselves. 'Oh little town of Bethlehem, Without a city wall, Where our dear lord was crucified . . .'

'Crucified? Please everyone. Stop. Those aren't the words at all.'

It was no good, they couldn't help it. They might as well sing as they felt. A carol for a birth, a lament for a death made no difference if you were expressing feelings. Their future held no Warden but Loveliness was restored. She was getting her promised outing, she'd see Daddie's other charity in the West Country with the residents instead of Daddie. His favourite song had been 'Stardust'. She liked this one best.

The last time they'd been in the red Ford they'd worn their caps and boots after the shopping trip. They'd never wear them again. The hankies were useful though, particularly now. They wanted to see the Twilight. Hounds were everyone's favourite, silky long-legged beasts, not like that mastiff at Hillside. The persons looking after the dogs might give them some elevenses. Tim wasn't hungry now he had Sylvie, the world was his wedding-cake, he'd not need pies again. He imagined the person in charge of the dogs might be a retired cook who liked making dinners for dogs. Sylvie had the road map. They were nearly there.

The gate of the Twilight Rest Centre was wrought iron, delicately chased. The walls round it were capped with snow, beginning to melt in the sun. It fell with watery thuds. The gate hinge squeaked, startling the dogs. The older residents put their hands to their ears, the barking was so loud. Each dog had a kennel on a rectangle of snow-slushed green. They peered from their pens as the residents walked up the path between lawns quite covered with pens. Dogs peered at them, pressing their muzzles against chicken wire, velvety eyes amazed. The residents weren't nervous, they were safe. They were in control here, no teeth

118

could get them, they could laugh. 'Hal-loo.'

'Don't make them more excited. They all look very old.' Sylvie wanted to make a good impression with their party. If only they would care more about what people thought. The residents owned nothing, they cared for no party or cause. Such childishness could be annoying. They looked better now than in Ireland, pink-cheeked, smelling of soap, though their clothes were raggy and soiled. Loveliness pulled herself as tall as she could.

'Hounds are nervous creatures' she said primly.

'How do you know, clever dick? When did you last meet one? Now then, don't start a tantrum.'

Too late, Loveliness stamped a galosh at Cap. There was a good deal she knew that they didn't. Daddie had respected her brain. She was tired of being belittled, she was better than any of them. Daddie understood this. He knew.

The door under the porch lantern opened. A tall lady stood there. She wore a yellow plait reaching to her waist. She stared at them, one hand on her velvet hip. She had mauve-painted eyelids under black-painted brows. She widened her eyes.

'Madam, are you in charge here? We've come on an official call.'

'Don't tell me, let me guess. You're Henry's down-and-outs from St Harmony. Right?'

'Henry? I take it you mean Warden Hemm, your employer, that is your . . . ex . . .' Tim fumbled for words. How overfamiliar she was, referring to Hemm as Henry. Hemm surely wouldn't have called them down-and-outs, though he may have thought it at times. He threw out his chest, filled with protectiveness. He'd protect Harmony, fight for them and Sylvie for the rest of his life if need be. How could Hemm have employed such a painted person to care for those silky dogs? Those clothes, those trousers, the face of her.

'Employer? Hubby you mean. I'm Henry Hemm's wife.

119

Now then, we're introduced. You're Tim aren't you? You must be Sylvie? What's up? Got a message?' She waved her wedding ring in their faces.

They didn't flinch, though Cap blinked. Tim, man of the world, understood. He got the picture. Hemm had had a weakness for the fairer sex, had liked variety. He'd even had eyes and ideas about his own dear wife until he, the husband, had stepped in. Hemm loved the dwarf too well, unwisely. He'd had eyes and ideas about this creature, he'd married her. That was *her* price. Hemm had a right to a wife. This particular wife was so crude, a bold and common creature. You would expect a wife of Hemm's to be middle-aged, clothed sensibly in dark garments, like Sister Cecilia. But she was more like a stripper in that tight rude blouse.

The other men didn't notice anything special. It took more than a lady with yellow hair and thin clothes to surprise them. They were used to unusual alliances, strange partnerships. What matter who married who? They wanted a bit of food. Loveliness sucked her thumbs noisily. Cap picked her up again.

'Well now, that's grand news. My apologies, Mrs Hemm. Warden Hemm said nothing to us. A dark horse was our Hemm. What do you think, Sylvie? A married man all the time. I presume you are in charge of the staff here, Mrs Hemm?'

'Yes, dear. I *am* the staff. You're quite right about Henry. Tight with the information is Henry.'

'Prepare for sad news. I . . . we have a shock for you.'

'Out with it. Cough it up.'

'Hemm has died. Early this a.m. We returned from a trip to Ireland. And . . . er . . . that's all. He's dead.'

Loveliness screwed her eyes up again, sucking her thumbs loudly. She wouldn't cry at this moment, she must hear what was said. Daddie, bemedalled and dead, hadn't told her this. They were right, he did keep secrets.

'What did you just say? Hen? My other half? Not my

Hen, he can't be dead?'

'I'm afraid he is, Mrs Hemm.'

'He was my Daddie,' Loveliness said softly.

'Daddie? He was my man. He couldn't just leave me flat. Oh no. No.' She put her wedding ring to her painted mouth.

'I'm afraid he has. Stroke very probably. He wasn't young, poor man.'

'Not so old either. He may have been a bit naughty sometimes. But he was all I had. We thought the world of each other. Oh no. Oh.'

'Daddie. Daddie.'

'Madam. I mean Mrs Hemm. Your husband died bravely. He had beliefs, he taught his residents a proper way of life. He loved people, he loved human nature.'

'He loved dogs, that I do know. He had some funny ways.'

'Yes. Well. Sylvie and I were wondering about the future, the immediate future I mean. He left no instructions. As his wife you'll have plans no doubt, you can tell us what we should do.'

'Where is Hen now?'

'We left Sole with the remains.'

'I ought to go to him.'

'He was a fine man. He kept his own counsel.'

'I ought to know that, didn't I? Tight with the info was Hen.'

'Daddie.'

'That's enough, Loveliness.' It was the second time that Tim had spoken directly to Loveliness. Until the future was more settled he must stay in charge. He must get used to addressing them personally, they must get used to him. When Hemm had breathed his last they'd looked instinctively at him. They needed a man at the top, a man with a wife better still. He smiled at Loveliness who had withstood jealousy. Hemm's wife must have come as a shock to the poor little casualty. Mrs Hemm must come back, her place was at Harmony. Might she want to close Harmony down? Might she prefer the dogs? He wouldn't think about it.

'I fancied meeting you only this morning. We've not been so long wed. Hen liked to keep his charities apart. It's dead quiet here. The dogs make a noise, otherwise it's dead. Come on in.'

She had sherry in the kitchen. They watched her pour the golden drink. Warden's strictest rule was being broken on the day of his death. Mrs Hemm said look on it as medicine, she often did, so did Hen. They enjoyed it, sipping it, except for Mac who gollupped, holding his glass for more. Mrs Hemm said anyone with such broad shoulders needed extra strength. Every put a shy hand out.

'We had a beautiful drive through the snow. Come back, Mrs Hemm. We'll help you to take a good heart.' He didn't want to show his gums, he tried to stand straight, man to woman. She smelled of dogs mixed with sherry. She took his hand, gripping it in both hers.

'You understand. I can tell. Hen was a lonely man. Some people are born lonely, you can't help how you're born, I was his wife, I know.'

Tim handed her a hanky. She evidently had feelings under that shallow face. She'd probably used Hemm, like everybody else. Naturally she missed him now. There was no need to speak of the fearful discoveries of this morning. The past was dead. Burned. His heart had gone out to Sylvie after all her pains, starting those files. How much had Sylvie felt for Hemm? Had she ever reciprocated his early interest? This sherry was pleasant, he had to admit, a semi-sweetish brand. Thoughtful of Mrs Hemm, she was trying to welcome them.

'Now then, what is your name, pet?'
'Loveliness. Loveliness Marker.'
'Thought so. Poor tiny mite.'

Cap whispered into the ear under the shiny yellow plait.

'Shame. Still, these things only matter as much as you let them. I've worked myself under the big top. I've done variety too.'

'Show business?' Loveliness was off again. Her tongue babbled. She spoke of her days of glory, how she'd worn white swansdown, rode in a coach. She'd flown to the moon, as well as visiting rabbit land. Those days were the loveliest of her life. It was a delight to find someone who understood. Daddie had shown great interest, but he wasn't here any more, and . . . What was the lady's name please? Tell.

'Gloria. I had my own spot. Poodles. I had them night and day in my van. Trained them, taught them somersaults. They had their own doggy cars, plus I made their clothes. I topped the bill till I met up with Hen.'

While Gloria spoke of her show business days Loveliness was muttering, recalling the captions under her pictures. The prettiest, the one she preferred was 'Sweet and Loveliness goes moon riding, flying to the man of her dreams'. She liked the sherry drink. No one could rob a memory.

'Hen wanted me for Twilight. He put a lot of himself into here. You can't mix poodles with hounds, I let my doggies go. But I liked the ring. 'The country here is cold. Dead quiet, week in week out.' Snow made her feel old. Twilight was cold alone. She was truly alone now, no more weekends with Hen. What would happen next?'

Sylvie spoke. 'Look, Gloria, Warden was a good boss to me, I worked for him for years. We need help. Come back to St Harmony. Can you leave now? Can you leave the dogs?'

'Not really. I could put them to bed now. They most probably won't notice.'

'Then do. St Harmony needs you today.' Sylvie asked if Warden had other relatives, if he had any friends. The residents were her real concern. Innocents soon forgot sorrow.

They had forgotten Warden's misdoings, had probably forgotten his death. Gloria was new blood, excitement, new life. They eyed her as if she were an angel pouring them milk of paradise. Gloria crooked her little finger over her glass. She'd add zest to the funeral. A widow would give it style.

'I had no one but him, *really*. I'll come back now. The dogs will manage. Hen would want it.'

'He would, Gloria. He would.' Sylvie looked at her thoughtfully. If Gloria could mother Loveliness, Cap might have time for her. She'd missed their old talks lately. Cap had been least surprised about Warden because of her knowledge of men. But he'd suffered, paid the price, died. Gloria had loved him. She would have them now.

'I always missed a family,' she said happily, patting her eyes again.

'Say goodbye to Daddie,' Loveliness would enjoy showing Gloria how pretty he looked, with his medal and the tree at his feet. She wanted to show her scrapbooks to Daddie's circus wife.

'Don't forget me, Babe. You need looking after. You always will, I bet.' Cap wasn't taking a back seat just yet. Gloria might have been Warden's better half, she was nothing else yet. Just because she'd been in show business Loveliness and the men stared as if she were a bit of cake or a fairy. Silly sods, like all men, easily impressed.

'Don't we all need a bit of looking after?' Gloria smiled her teeth at Every again.

'May we assist with the animals' dinner, Madam?'

'Ta dear. That is kind, *really*.'

Cooking for the hounds was messy work. The meat was horse steaks, dyed green. You boiled it, stirring in oddments at the end. Gloria hated cooking.

'Let me, Gloria. I like handling knives.'

Mac sliced and chopped for Gloria, throwing cubed meat into the pot. He spoke of his ambition to be a knife thrower.

She said she'd partnered a knife thrower once, human target. Oh she'd had her thrills. Hen's weekends were the only excitement since leaving the big top. She poked in the pot, adding some old carrots. 'You know how I feel, don't you? Easterners are so sensitive.'

'Veree. Very,' Mr Silk answered, handing her a spoon.

She didn't cook for herself often. Did they fancy some of the stew? The residents smiled. Their angel was offering them food. Mr Silk shook his head.

'Vegetables better for soul.'

'You're so right, dear. Meat taints the system. I love the East myself. I'll go there one day most probably.'

The rest touched their lips with their spoons.

'Well really. I can't. These are dogs' basins,' Sylvie whispered to Tim.

'Don't touch it, darling,' he answered, pouring her bowl into his own. If she'd only appealed to him years ago. He felt gentle, protective, sure. They'd stock up at the supermarket on their way home. Sylvie must have proper meals.

Before they left Gloria gave the hounds aspirin. They helped her poke the pills through the chicken wire into the dogs' jaws. They were very old, with white whiskers round their mouths and rather shaky limbs. They took the pills as easily as sweets, going to their kennels after.

The Twilight was colder, quieter, with the dogs silenced by aspirin and sleep. They closed the wrought-iron gates. Snow still plopped from the walls. They whispered a last 'Hal-loo' before piling into the old red Ford.

Gloria insisted on sitting in the back. Sylvie must stay with Tim, she wanted to cuddle with the residents, to hear about their hopes, their dreams, their fears. They were her family already.

'Tim paints, you know. And Sylvie cooks and sews. We want to fix the house, make it more weatherproof. I collect things, I help out.' Cap wouldn't be out of it. If they wanted Gloria let her come. If you can't lick 'em, join 'em.

125

Silly sods.

Tim and Sylvie spoke together. They might go collective if Gloria agreed. They'd work hard, expand. Use the top floor for more residents, take in their pets as well. They might even try another Irish trip, with Gloria. They saw a shining future, a clearer way ahead. They sang with the others in the back. 'Oh little town of Bethlehem, Without a city wall.' They smiled at each other. Absurd. They laughed then.

❧ Thirteen

ST HARMONY CO-OPERATIVE

Grand Easter Fair
Dart contests and puppet shows.
Exhibition of yoga.
Stalls for old and new clothing.
Bric-a-brac.
Home-made cakes and wines.
Portraits of animals by our resident artist. Bring your pets.
